THE SUPERHERO FORMULA

Starts with You

Indu Balakrishnan

ISBN
Paperback 979-8-89186-787-1
Hardcase 979-8-89929-912-4

CONTENTS

PART I: MY SECRET FRIEND

FOREWORD

Stories shape us. They spark curiosity, teach us values, and—at their best—make us pause and reflect. The Superhero Formula does exactly that. Through the twin journeys of Raha and Agni, Indu Balakrishnan invites young readers into a world where imagination meets responsibility. Here, courage is rooted in empathy, and superpowers take second place to inner strength.

What's especially compelling is that this book doesn't offer easy answers or one-size-fits-all heroes. It asks children to question what's right, explore what it means to care deeply, and reflect on their role in society. Not just as recipients of rights, but as active citizens with duties. Few books walk that fine line between fun and philosophy, but Indu manages it with heart, humor, and a touch of science fiction.

There are moments in the story where the protagonist's sense of adventure takes her into situations that are bold, perhaps a little too bold for real life. Venturing alone into a forest to crack a smuggling case, for instance, isn't something young readers should try themselves. But that is the beauty of fiction. It gives children the freedom to imagine the "what if," while still offering gentle reminders about the boundaries that keep us safe.

I've had the privilege of working closely with Indu for over five years. She brings relentless energy, good intent, and an infectious enthusiasm to everything she does. She is brilliant with children, deeply thoughtful about society, and incredibly committed to making a difference. This book feels like a natural extension of who she is. It is imaginative, grounded, and filled with hope.

If you are a young reader, this book will take you on an adventure. If you are a parent, teacher, or mentor, this is a wonderful conversation starter. Real superheroes aren't born in comic books. They are shaped by values, choices, and voices like Indu's.

And as her friend, I'm cheering her on as she brings this beautiful story into the world. May it inspire many young minds and take her on the fulfilling journey she truly deserves.

– Ganapathy Sankarabaaham, Founder & CEO,
Vajra Global Consulting Services LLP and XITE Create

BOOK REVIEWS

In this heroic and inspirational book, Indu Balakrishnan explores the strengths of today's Youth of India - who they are, and where as responsible citizens, they can take their country in the future. The tone of the novel is set right from the beginning, as the two stories involved take the readers to a world where fictitious events complement non-fiction, interesting things unfold in the invisible, cosmic events are seen in a new perspective, and the ultimate metamorphosis of the two characters, Agni and Raha, transforming them into superhumans, adds a new dimension to life and how it should be lived.

This book is as enjoyable as it is stimulating - an outstanding literary narrative that inspires modern minds to change and take meaningful action that can shape the future.

I would recommend THE SUPERHERO FORMULA to anyone who is interested in the history and future of our Indian Constitution.

– Daffenee Rodgers, Principal,
Bala Vidya Mandir Senior Secondary School, Chennai

I read a lot of books, and I can honestly say this one is one of my all-time favorites! It perfectly combines things that kids like me can relate to with fresh, exciting ideas. The story was super fun and packed with adventures that kept me hooked the whole time. I really liked how the characters felt like real people, and the book taught important lessons without ever being boring. I would definitely recommend it to anyone looking for a great read!

– Nivedita M Pillai

A 13-year-old book lover and budding author

There is a misconception we labour under that our rights and duties are only those which are given to us by the law. In reality, nothing could be farther from the truth. Our rights as humans and our duties to one another are building blocks on which society forms and civilisations develop. To ignore them, not imbibe them, or not recognise them is the greatest disservice anyone can do. Life, much like time, is forward-looking. It is for this reason that youngsters should know about their rights and duties because they are the inheritors of the earth that has been left for them.

– Thriyambak Kannan,
Partner, Khaitan and Co.

As a mental health practitioner for over 8 years, this book and its contents resonated with me more deeply than I can express. One of my roles includes working with vulnerable children and families who have been exposed to adverse life experiences such as poverty, family violence, neglect, lack of education, and basic needs. Intergenerational trauma is a real thing, which means every generation requires the appropriate type of support and care to be the best versions of themselves. The children of today are the leaders of tomorrow, and therefore, have a right to live in an environment where they feel heard, seen, loved, and cared for. Children and teenagers are increasingly vulnerable, and any negative impact on their mental health can have long-term consequences. Therefore, every child should have a voice to be able to advocate for themselves as well as positive role models growing up.

This book hits the right spot, speaking about the current challenges in society that children experience when they are denied equality, human rights, and an environment to thrive in.

It is evident from reading the book that Indu is a passionate social worker who cares deeply not just about her own family and friends, but also for those in society. The contents of this book are not to be missed.

Very empowering read!

– Eshwari Gorsia
Mental Health Practitioner

ACKNOWLEDGEMENTS

To my amazing family - Bala, Vaishnavi, Niranjan, and Marvel (the coolest hot-tempered cat ever) - thanks for the constant support, endless fun and for always being there, especially when I was lost.

Thank you, Amma, for always believing I can do anything I set my mind to.

And Eshwari, my wonderful sister (+built-in best friend + confidante + partner-in-crime).

Basically, couldn't have done it without you all. Seriously.

You're the best. End of story (well, almost!).

Thank you, Marvel and DC Universes, for inspiring the super hero love in me.

Thank you to the creators of the Indian Constitution and to all who work so hard to make its tenets a reality.

To every reader who's opened these pages and let the stories live within them – thank you! It's a wonder beyond words.

– Indu Balakrishnan

ABOUT THE AUTHOR

You don't need a cape to be a hero. You just need to believe in doing your part for the greater good.

Meet Indu Balakrishnan: future journalist, passionate social worker, Montessori-trained educator, and lifelong superhero fan. Inspired by epic adventures where everyday people discover unbelievable powers, she writes to show young readers that real-world heroism starts within.

Indu's love for children and her deep understanding of how young minds learn and grow allow her to connect effortlessly with her audience. She believes that every child carries the potential to shape a better world—and that the seeds of change are planted through small, courageous choices made every day.

True progress begins with the rule of law —the simple but powerful idea that individuals, institutions, and the government must all play by the same rules. Rooted in a strong belief in fairness and shared responsibility, Indu champions a world where governments and citizens walk hand in hand toward progress. She trusts that governments strive for the well-being of their people, but knows that true, lasting change also depends on citizens stepping up—respecting the Constitution, protecting the rights of humans and animals alike, and ensuring that justice and kindness are everyday acts.

With a pen in one hand and a heart full of hope, Indu invites you to explore the thrilling balance between rights, responsibilities, and the choices that define who we become.

This book is just the beginning. Are you ready to find out what you're made of?

WHY THIS BOOK NEEDS YOU!

Human rights and the Indian Constitution are deeply meaningful to me because they represent the foundation of justice, equality, and dignity for every individual. With a master's degree in Human Rights and Duties, I feel a strong responsibility to use my voice and skills to inspire change. Through the power of storytelling, I aim to connect with the youth of today by blending superheroes and adventure—creating characters that reflect real world struggles and triumphs.

My goal is not just to entertain but to create awareness and a sense of responsibility in young minds toward building a better India. Writing is my way of creating impact. As I nurture my growth as a social worker and journalist, I aspire to turn these words into meaningful action—transforming ideas into movements that promote social justice and empowering communities through advocacy.

And this cannot be done without you.

– Indu Balakrishnan

PART I

MY SECRET FRIEND

PROLOGUE

Sometimes, all it takes is a slightly different viewpoint to make you realize how little you actually know. It can be pretty humbling. It's a constant reminder that there's always more to learn and discover. It can really throw you for a loop! You often live within the boundaries of your own beliefs and perspectives, assuming them to be the sole truth. Two plus two is always four. But then, if you take a glass of water at 20°C and mix it with another glass at the same temperature, the combined temperature will not be 40°C. It doesn't work that way.

The Eureka moment could come at any time. The 2 + 2 'aha moment.' It might really surprise you and make you question everything you thought you knew. Suddenly, you see there's a different way to look at things.

But wait, that's not the point of this ramble. I didn't mean to start with a scientific theory. This story is anything but that. Well, it most definitely isn't Marvel or DC. But this is sci-fi with a twist, and I'd love for you to be part of it.

Here's something that might shock you. For instance, where do you think I am right now? Sipping juice on the beach? Sitting in the park with a burger in my hand? Nope. I wish I were. I don't know how I ended up here. I mean, I do…

That was a rhetorical question.

So, what's happening? I am speaking to you from inside a small, windowless room. I can smell the scent of the river nearby and the woods. The hooting owls break the otherwise complete silence. The silence is deafening, and my heart is hammering against my ribs like a trapped bird. Easily at 200 beats per minute.

If I hadn't been tied up (in the literal sense! I'm not busy), I might have found this serenity relaxing. Yes, I've been kidnapped, and I'm waiting for my friend to come and rescue me. However, it has been an unusual 15 minutes of deathly quiet. Excuse the word deathly. No, I am not being dramatic. This is very unnerving, considering she's **always** around me, filling the air with her ceaseless chatter, wisecracks, and advice. To give you a bit of a back story, I'll tell you who I am talking about. And why I would expect her here. Out of all the people in my life.

She has been my best friend and partner-in-crime for as long as I can remember. Her name is Raha. She has always been with me, wherever I went, whatever the time or place. For so long, I have never questioned the absurdity of it. Her absence, in fact, was what raised my eyebrows.

To tell you more about our friendship, she was like my soul sister. We loved to talk about anything and everything under the sun and beyond. One of my favorite topics was the universe and how we saw it.

I remembered one of our earlier conversations. "You know, I've been thinking about life, the universe, and everything in it," I had said.

"Ah, the eternal questions. Go on, my philosopher friend," she had smirked.

"What's the meaning of it all? Why are we here? What's the purpose of life?"

"Well, it's like this. Life is a bit like pizza. You see, it's round, often cheesy, and you always want another slice."

I recollected chuckling at the analogy. I did like pizza, and I loved cheese. I would always ask for another slice. And life is indeed a circle. What goes around comes around. Life **is** like a pizza. Wow! How had I not seen that?

"And what about the universe? It's so huge and mysterious," I had asked, grinning at her.

"The universe is like a teenager's room. You never know what's hiding in each corner, and there are so many unanswered questions." Her answers were always prompt, to the point, and profound. Like she knew what I was going to ask.

I thought about it. She was right—questions you probably don't even want answered in the first place.

She is my best friend, sounding board, and the person who makes my life brighter.

Oh, and did I mention that she's invisible? That's right; no one has ever seen Raha, not even me. I only feel her presence. I can proudly say that I am the one who named her. It means 'peace of mind.' Why did I pick that name for her? Because she soothes my nerves and keeps me centered and grounded as and when needed.

Strangely, she has never had a name. Or she refused to tell me. Hmm… that's rude. Why would she do that? I once even asked her how she would get ready and put on makeup if she were invisible. I never quite got a reply.

I'm sorry. With my life in danger, I should not digress.

Let me reassure you—this is not a plot from a horror movie. On the contrary, she's my best friend, an intimate confidante who knows me inside and out. My philosopher and guide. We share a remarkable connection. Our minds work in tandem. We harbor the same outlandish ideas and irrational fears, share similar whimsical fancies, and possess an insatiable passion for science. Thanks to her influence, I developed a penchant for taking things apart to understand their inner workings. This curiosity often came at a cost. I paid dearly for my inquisitive nature and failed to repair many of my dismantled creations like my great grandfather's clock, an antique iron box, a digital thermometer, and countless other objects. Oh well!

Raha was also why I could find humor in my darkest moments and courage in the face of danger. Due to her invisible presence (an oxymoron probably never used before), I discovered a world beyond reality. She showed me that life is not all black and white, that there's magic in science, and that friendship can travel beyond the boundaries of the tangible world.

Now, in my confinement, where time stretches into eternity, I yearn for her presence more than ever. Something was amiss, and I couldn't shake the feeling that her absence had something to do with it.

Scratch that—it had everything to do with it.

I had a zillion questions in my head. Why was she silent? Did she not know that I needed her help? Or didn't she know how to help me? Would I ever find a way out?

The fear of danger is 10,000 times more terrifying than the danger itself.

And I was terrified right now.

You feel a tad lost too, don't you? I suppose it's time to tell you more about us.

Cut-scene.

[A cut-scene is a brief, cinematic interlude that provides a crucial backstory or advances the plot. You're likely familiar with this term from video games or films like Jumanji. I tend to ramble, don't I?]

It was a meeting that would change everything. She saved my life the very first time we met. (Ok, she didn't save my life per se, but that's how I saw it back then). It is all a matter of perspective, isn't it? The truth is that just because it happened in your head doesn't mean it isn't real.

The mind is mighty but can also be quite vulnerable. Troublesome situations bring about negative responses such as fear. Now, there is nothing wrong with fear. It is a natural response to an unfamiliar situation. That is when faith plays a huge role. It gets you going when nothing else can. It removes the demons that you have created for yourselves, the ones that stop you from getting where you want to go.

HOW WE MET

My first conscious encounter with Raha occurred during my first year of school. She claims to have been a part of my life for much longer, but my earliest memories don't extend that far back. Perhaps I was too young to grasp her presence at the time. Regardless, this particular encounter stands out vividly, leaving me profoundly terrified—in every conceivable sense of the word.

You know how it goes. Sometimes, when you read a well-written sentence, you close the book and let it linger in your thoughts. This incident had a similar effect on me. The scene would replay in my mind, vividly and involuntarily, whenever I experienced a surge of fear.

So, this is what happened. I was fast asleep in my room when I saw something dart across the floor. In my head, I could hear myself let out a blood-curdling scream. But, in reality, nothing came out. Not a peep. I couldn't muster the strength to call out to my mother, nor could I find the courage to leave my bed. A wave of utter helplessness washed over me.

Fun fact: Fear can produce so much adrenaline that you can lift a car. It can generate additional strength, focus, and clarity. But it can also freeze you. Freezing is the fight-or-flight on hold, where you prepare to protect yourself. It is your body's way of reacting to danger. When you feel scared or threatened, your body gets ready to either fight the scary thing or run away from it. It's a primal survival mechanism designed to protect you in the face of perceived danger.

Imagine seeing a big, scary dog. Your heart may race, you might sweat, and your muscles will tense. This is your body preparing to fight or run away from the dog.

Funny how that works.

But, in that moment of darkness and dread, I felt it—a gentle hand softly grasping mine. Suddenly, everything seemed better. The darkness was still there, but my fear had vanished. I was no longer alone—and I don't mean it in a creepy way, like in the horror movies.

Raha whispered in my ear, "Do not worry. It's nothing."

Strangely, I believed her… because how could I not? I felt an overwhelming sense of comfort wash over me. My pulse slowed down, increasing the levels of endorphins. The body produces them to help relieve pain, reduce stress, and improve one's mood. I felt safe. That feeling had never gone away until this moment.

She had become my security blanket.

Raha's mantra was, "Walk like you have 10 people behind you."

You know what? I didn't need anyone to watch my back because I had her. She made me feel safe and at ease. No one had ever made me feel this way in my entire life. I mean, not counting my parents, of course. Since then, her hand has held mine several times and guided me through moments of doubt and fear. You must have heard the saying, 'Friendships, even the best of them, are frail things. One drifts apart.' This one defied all odds, and I couldn't have asked for more.

My schooling was pure joy because of her. Raha was like the mischievous lamb that Mary had, following me to school every day. Now, that was definitely against the rules. The rhyme made it very clear, too. The catch was that no one could see her. I did tell you that she was invisible, didn't I? Yes, I couldn't see her either. But I felt her presence next to me all the time. She felt like my kindred spirit. If I ever needed to know that she was around and hadn't walked off into the sunset, she'd give my hand a little squeeze. That's how she let me know she was right there with me. I'd tap out the Morse Code on a table or wall when I needed reassurance. It was three short taps followed by three long taps, and three short taps once again. And she'd respond in a flash, with a touch that spoke volumes.

Of course, when we were alone, the floodgates of conversation would burst open. I would tell her about my wildest dreams and silliest fears, and she would respond with wisdom that could rival any grown-up. She was my walking-talking diary, i.e., an interactive one.

Here's the kicker: While I found our talks incredibly enlightening, they usually ended with her cracking a joke that would have me laughing until my sides hurt. It was like having my very own invisible stand-up comedian, and boy, did she keep me amused.

With her by my side, every day at school became an adventure filled with laughter and endless pranks.

Raha introduced me to the true essence of science—not the rote memorization of plant parts or chemical elements that characterized my school curriculum. No. She showed me that science was a never-ending journey where you could explore the same concept from countless angles. That lesson changed how I looked at the world forever.

"Why is our syllabus all about memorizing facts and figures? It seems so boring," I remember complaining once.

I had a lot of studying to do for a test, and I felt this took the fun out of learning. We should **want** to learn. It should not be like a chore or a checkbox that we need to tick in order to qualify for the next grade.

"Ah, but science starts with that. You need to know the basics. Just like you need to know the alphabet before you start writing words and sentences. Like your warm-up exercises before you start playing your game. But having said that, science is so much more!" she replied.

"Really? How so?"

"Well. Science isn't just about memorizing facts. It is about asking the right questions. That's how it all begins."

"So, what are we waiting for? Let's go!" I shrieked.

"We start right here, right now—biology, physics, and chemistry. Go back to the drawing board. You'll see that science is the answer to anything you want to ask."

With her idea firmly planted in my head, I began to approach every subject curiously by using the '5 Whys' technique. Whether it was a leaf in the garden, a distant galaxy and the possibility of life on it, or a roaring dinosaur from the past, I tried to give it a new perspective.

As I read, I learned. I studied not just for marks but to look at the bigger picture, and I tried to apply it in real life. The kitchen was a fantastic place to start. I began experimenting with baking, exploring the chemical reactions that transformed flour, sugar, and eggs into delicious cakes and bread. I noticed how heat changes food in different ways. When you boil an egg, it becomes hard. But when you boil a potato, it becomes soft. My kitchen was my lab. My father gave me a fire extinguisher, just in case. He didn't mind the madness as long as I cleaned up the mess.

I became known as one of the most adventurous girls in class, always eager to ask questions, go beyond the textbook, and see the world through the lens of science. Einstein once said, "Creativity is intelligence having fun." Thanks to Raha, who brought the magic of science into my life, I was doing just that.

The other day, we were talking about DNA.

"DNA seems like a bunch of random letters and codes to me. How do we crack it?" I asked.

"Well, think of DNA as the ultimate instruction manual for life. It's like the most detailed recipe book ever written."

"A recipe book? How so?"

"Imagine each DNA strand is like a recipe. Each recipe contains instructions for creating a unique living being. It's like having a formula for every living thing on Earth."

"That's amazing! So, is DNA like the secret code that creates life itself?"

"Exactly! It is the blueprint that shapes everything, from the huge oak tree to a tiny ladybug. And guess what? We can learn to read and understand these recipes to interpret the mysteries of life!" she explained.

"Can it help cure and eventually prevent cancer?" I pondered.

She didn't answer, but I am sure she smiled proudly. She loved it when I let my imagination run wild.

If you've got enough nerve, you sort of start thinking that anything is possible. With Raha by my side around the clock, I didn't feel scared at all. Her presence filled me with courage and a boundless sense of possibility. For us, the limits of imagination and discovery seemed to stretch endlessly. The school lab was at my disposal, thanks to the special permission I received from the principal herself.

I observed a peculiar pattern in our interactions. Raha knew what to tell me and what I should discover on my own. However, I never asked her how she knew so much. In fact, I never asked her for her backstory. It was always about me. My dreams. My adventure. My career. My decisions. She made sure that I took the right path. She believed that our choices showed what we truly are, more than our skills or talent. After all, it's not who we are but what we do that defines us, yes?

Now, as I miss her, I can't help but wonder…What if…

MY BACKSTORY

Oh, did I tell you? I lived in Kabini. My parents worked at a wildlife conservatory, and our home was literally in the forest. A river flowed nearby, its waters reducing the temperatures around the year and giving the place a very resort-y look.

Now, for the best part. I was often home alone. We had a cook come in and prepare food for the day. She also packed sandwiches and French fries twice a week so that I could take them with me when I studied under this very large tree in the forest. I loved learning and could do it in a really fun location. Life was good!

The days rarely passed without incident. Once, I stumbled upon an injured bird in my usual study spot. Its wing appeared to be hurt, and it could not fly. I tiptoed towards it. It seemed scared but didn't fly away. It couldn't. Carefully, I extended my hand, and it hopped onto my palm.

"We won't hurt you, little one. We're here to help," I reassured the bird.

It might have asked me why I spoke in the first person plural if it had understood English. I made a tiny splint with great care from twigs and leaves to secure the bird's injured wing. Raha and I found a safe, cozy spot in the forest and made a small nest.

"There, little bird. You're safe now," Raha whispered, her voice a gentle murmur in the stillness of the woods.

The bird, startled by the unexpected sound, jerked violently. This was unprecedented. Never before had anyone else heard Raha's voice. The realization struck me with the force of a thunderbolt: Raha was not merely a figment of my imagination. Her existence was undeniable. However, I knew better than to press for answers. The time for revelations, I felt, had not yet arrived.

We watched over the bird as it rested and healed. Days passed, and the bird's wing slowly mended.

"Look! It's getting better," I said joyfully.

"Our little friend will soon be able to soar in the skies again," Raha replied triumphantly.

When the day for the bird to take flight arrived, we removed the splint and cheered it on as it soared high into the skies.

Did it sound like I was having a lot of fun? All play and no study? Well, it most definitely was not like that.

Let me tell you a little bit more about myself. You must be wondering about my routine. I did do a lot more than play in the jungle with Raha. This was just fun we had over the weekend. My weekdays were busy.

The school bus picked me up every morning, and the trip to school was quite long. The ride might have been boring to the ordinary, but I had Raha with me, remember? (If you are wondering, "Oh, are we back to talking about Raha?" let me gently remind you that the title of this story is 'My Secret Friend' ☺)

Raha would give me a running commentary of what was happening and crack random jokes, and I'd be busy trying not to giggle. Mind you, people found talking and laughing to themselves are not looked at kindly.

There were just a handful of kids on my school bus. I lived on the outskirts of the city, and only a few kids lived near me. While they slept or stared out of the window, lost in thought, I was engaged in very silent but lively conversations with my invisible friend. It was during these rides that our bond grew stronger. Little did I know that these moments would shape not only our friendship but my idea of a career in science.

My father, a long-standing member of the State Forest Department, worked tirelessly to protect the forests and wildlife surrounding our home. He and his colleagues were the first responders in any situation involving wild animals, and their passion for conservation ran deep. A poster of The Wildlife Protection Act, 1972, took center stage in his room. It was a daily reminder of the laws and responsibilities safeguarding India's wild animals, birds, and plant species. The Act also protects elephants as a Schedule I species. The State Forest Department can seize illegally owned elephants and rehabilitate them in elephant camps. In this forest, they took priority.

On the other hand, my mother had initially pursued a career as a criminal lawyer. However, her love for my father and her support for his work changed her priorities. She decided to shift her specialization to environmental law, aligning her expertise with his mission to protect the natural world. Together, they made a formidable team that was dedicated to preserving the wilderness surrounding us in Kabini.

My parents' jobs kept them occupied throughout the day. With their responsibilities and commitments, they had little time to spare for pretty much anything else. As a result, I often had to fend for myself, but as you already know, I was never truly alone.

Often, my parents (especially my mom) felt guilty. But being alone most of the time gave me the confidence that I could take care of myself, and I would tell her that what she was doing was amazing. Sometimes, it felt like I was the one taking care of my parents. I would heat the dinner and keep it ready when they came home. I would also set the table and make the occasional milkshake or brownie in the mug for those moments of indulgence. Yup, I had it all under control.

Did you know that 'mom guilt' is a real thing? This phenomenon is a pervasive and often overwhelming feeling that plagues many mothers. It's that nagging sense that they are not doing enough for their children or are somehow failing as a parent. So, apart from saving the natural environment, I was on a mission to make sure that my parents were also well taken care of.

Raha filled my life with fun and laughter. Weekends, in particular, were a delight as the four of us (according to my parents, there were three of us) would venture deep into the forest for long walks and explorations. As I mentioned earlier, fear never found a place in my heart.

The weeks flew by. School. Homework. Some TV time. Reading books. A little workout along with studying for tests. This happened almost every other week. And then, of course, we had fun bantering with each other.

"Have you heard about the legend of the ancient tree in the heart of the forest?" I asked during one of our brainstorming sessions while strolling through the jungle.

"Tell me more. Legends often hold secrets waiting to be discovered."

I couldn't resist sharing a story I'd heard from a fellow adventurer. "You see, there's a tale about a tree deep within these woods. They say it's older than time itself, its roots tangled with the very soul of the forest."

"Oh, that does sound fascinating. Very much like the Tree of Souls in the movie, 'Avatar.' What else have you heard about it?" she asked.

"Legend has it that the tree possesses magical properties. It's said that those who find it and decode its secrets will be granted one wish, but only if their heart is pure," I said animatedly.

"A wish from an ancient tree in the heart of the forest. What a captivating fantasy. Do you think it could be real?"

"Who knows? Maybe, just maybe, we'll stumble upon it. And if we do, we'll uncover the greatest secret of all—the secret of the universe," I said optimistically.

However, I could never zero in on what my wish would be. It's a good thing we never found the tree. What if I had wasted it on an unlimited supply of fat-free dark chocolates? That would have been nice, though.

I had a feeling she knew about the tree. I don't know how, but she seemed to know everything. Nevertheless, she always indulged me, patiently listening to my never-ending rambling.

When I reached Class 12, studying was a breeze, not just because I was a diligent student who attended classes religiously and stood first in class but because she was there to teach me. My parents always knew that I loved science. But what made them really proud was the fact that my love matched theirs and that I wanted to specialize in human rights and duties and eventually collaborate with them to conserve the natural world.

CHAPTER THREE

I OWN MY SECRET

I excelled in almost everything I put my mind to. Soon enough, I was praised for being a fabulous all-rounder. The accolades poured in, and I was the shining star of my school. I participated in inter-school events and won many trophies & medals. The problem was that I received all the credit, credit that I knew I did not entirely deserve. This weighed on my conscience, and I felt a growing urge—like an annoying itch—to be honest with my parents.

I vividly recall the day I gathered the courage to tell them the truth. I slowly but firmly confessed that I had an invisible friend who had been a massive part of my life. IKR. It sounded so weird. I should have played the conversation out in my head first. I would have laughed if someone had said that to me.

I can almost sense your disbelief. You've invested so much time in this story, and yet, the very core of it—my friendship with Raha—might seem utterly fantastical. But my parents… their reaction was far more unexpected than I could have ever imagined.

Tell me… Did you have trouble believing that I had such a friend?

Anyway.

"Mom, Dad, there's something I've wanted to tell you," I began nervously.

"What is it, sweetie?" Mom watched me struggle and added, "You know you can tell us anything."

FYI. Moms think they can handle anything and everything. They can. In time. But it takes a while. Until then, be ready. For anything.

"I… I have an invisible friend. Her name is Raha. She's been with me for as long as I can remember," I told them hesitantly.

Mom and Dad exchanged amused glances.

"An invisible friend? That's quite an imagination, kiddo," Dad chuckled.

"No, Dad, it's not just my imagination. She's real. She has helped me with my studies and given me advice, and we've had the most amazing conversations. She's my best friend. Really!"

I was determined to stand my ground and not be laughed at.

The conversation went back and forth. In a loop. Each party repeating the same thing but in different ways. Trying to convince the other.

"It's cute that you have an imaginary friend, dear. Lots of kids do. But you'll outgrow it," Mom said, attempting to take me seriously while making sure I wasn't too serious about it.

She had other concerns. How would I ever get admission into a good college? What will society think?

Parenting is tough, isn't it?

"No! Mom! Dad! You don't understand. She's not imaginary. She's been a part of my life, guiding me in so many ways," I said, frustrated.

Dad patted my head affectionately. "We appreciate your creativity, but it's time to focus on the real world, okay?"

My heart sank when I realized that my parents didn't take me seriously. "You don't believe me," I said, disheartened.

"Sweetie, it's just a phase. You'll see," Mom said gently.

My parents dismissed the conversation, leaving me feeling unheard, untrusted, and frustrated.

I was this close to telling them that she was in the room with us. But then, what if they called an exorcist? Yeah. Bad idea. I shut up immediately. It took immense self-control, but I did it without showing anything on my face. It is a skill, I tell you.

I tried sharing the secret with a couple of friends too, hoping to find someone who would believe me. However, they gave me strange looks too, clearly not comprehending my version of reality or the depth of my bond with Raha. I couldn't blame them entirely; I might have reacted similarly if our roles were reversed. Their skepticism, however, left me feeling isolated. I could not share this extraordinary aspect of my life with anyone else.

I grappled with the dilemma of revealing her existence to some more people. Eventually, I just stopped trying. It seemed easier to keep our unique bond a secret. However, as time passed, the weight of my silence began to wear on me. I couldn't bear it any longer, knowing she was the true genius, not me. Raha would hear me complain about it and tell me that it would all work out in the end. I would calm down until the next wave of guilt appeared. This cycle kept repeating.

After a while, we moved on. For the time being, at least.

Raha was there to assist me with my studies, to understand my homework, and to be present as my sounding board for crucial career decisions, along with the occasional whining. Together, we researched career paths, picked courses, and selected good colleges. I had my sights set on joining the forensics science department, a field that blended modern science with legal principles to analyze evidence and solve crimes. This type of investigation would be admissible in a court of law. The course would allow me to merge my passion for science with the pursuit of justice.

My passion was to eventually assist in building policies that helped build a stronger justice system, enabling the rule of law. The rule of law is the idea that everyone, including leaders, must follow the same laws. It's a fundamental principle that ensures a just and orderly society.

This is what I applied for.

Undergraduate Course in Forensic Science	
Course Name: Bachelor of Science (B.Sc.) in Forensic Science	
Duration: 3 years (6 semesters)	
Semester	Subjects covered
Semester 1	- Introduction to Forensic Science - Basics of Criminal Justice System - Principles of Chemistry - General Biology - Fundamentals of Physics
Semester 2	- Forensic Chemistry - Forensic Biology - Crime Scene Investigation - Physical Evidence Examination - Fundamentals of Criminal Law
Semester 3	- Forensic Toxicology - Forensic Pathology - Criminalistics - Criminal Investigation Techniques - Analytical Chemistry

Undergraduate Course in Forensic Science	
Semester 4	- Forensic Serology - Trace Evidence Analysis - Cyber Forensics - Advanced Forensic Techniques - Forensic Psychology
Semester 5	- Forensic Odontology - Forensic Entomology - DNA Analysis and Profiling - Forensic Document Examination - Medico-legal Ethics and Professionalism
Semester 6	- Forensic Anthropology - Forensic Photography - Forensic Statistics - Internship/Practical Training - Research Project and Dissertation

Raha and I would spend hours discussing it, and I became more reassured that this was where I was meant to be. Together, we dreamed of a future where we could contribute to deterring and solving crimes.

The burden of keeping our shared journey a secret became unbearable, and I knew I had to find a way to tell the truth to those who mattered the most to me. Everyone was applauding my achievements when Raha deserved the recognition more. It felt almost as crazy as mom guilt and as real.

The whole scene would have been quite funny if this hadn't happened to me. This was my last attempt at convincing my parents about my invisible friend. Yes, I can see why the plan seems ridiculous.

One weekend, we were seated at the kitchen table where we usually had our evening snacks. It was our family time. I had a stubborn look on my face and was ready to say my piece.

"Mom, Dad, I need to talk to you about something. It's about my invisible friend," I began nervously.

"Oh, not this again!" Mom responded irritably.

She wanted to believe me but was afraid of indulging my so-called fantasies. Dad exchanged a weary glance with her.

"We've been through this before. Your invisible friend is just a phase, right?" He was exasperated.

"No, it's not a phase. I talk to her all the time. Raha is real, and she has helped me so much," I said with conviction.

Mom and Dad looked at each other with alarm. Mom was afraid that Dad would lose his temper.

"This is getting serious. We need to do something about it now." Mom began to panic, trying to mitigate the situation before it flew out of control.

"Maybe it's time to see a therapist. They can help you understand what's going on," Dad offered.

My heart sank, and I realized that my parents' reaction was a mixture of anger, fear, and concern.

"You still don't believe me." I was disappointed.

"Sweetheart, it's not that we don't believe you. We're just worried about your emotional well-being," Mom said, her eyes filled with concern.

"We want to make sure you're okay. That's all," Dad added worriedly.

It was clear that they couldn't fathom the idea of an invisible friend being anything more than a figment of a child's imagination. To be fair, I wasn't even a child. I was a teen, for crying out loud! Teens didn't have such fantasies.

I quickly realized that some things were better left unspoken. The topic was dropped, but my parents watched me closely for several weeks afterward. I must have appeared like a ticking bomb to them—cute but potentially explosive at any moment. To ease their concerns, I consciously avoided talking about or to Raha whenever they were around. Gradually, they relaxed and believed that things had returned to normal or whatever they defined as normal.

COLLEGE

I passed my Class 12 board exams with flying colors and was admitted to the college of my dreams. While no one seemed surprised, no one celebrated quite like Raha. She was over the moon with excitement, and we decided to mark the occasion with a special celebration—a movie night featuring The Bone Collector.

The movie was a natural choice for aspiring forensic scientists. It revolved around a serial killer who left cryptic clues at crime scenes for a quadriplegic forensic criminology expert, Lincoln Rhyme, to solve. The bad guy was challenging the cops. Rhyme took the help of a quick-thinking policewoman named Amelia Donaghy to catch this bad guy. They always seemed to be running out of time as they attempted to solve the clues and save lives.

The lead characters in the movie had all the qualities I aspired for—the ability to make bold decisions in the face of danger, stomach any predicament with courage, and draw a clear line between the personal and the professional. It was a thrilling movie, and as the credits rolled, Raha and I sat in silence, appreciating science like never before. It was a celebration to remember, a tribute to our shared dreams, and a testament to our unbreakable bond.

Throughout the movie, I watched in awe as Amelia was called upon to venture into dark and dangerous places alone. Armed only with a flashlight and Rhyme's instructions in her ear (she was constantly on the phone with him as she fearlessly entered subterranean ratholes and abandoned factories). Cops were asked to stay away as she studied the crime scenes. This was to make sure that no evidence was disturbed or ruined.

As I watched her face these difficult situations with determined resolve, I couldn't help but feel a deep sense of admiration and kinship. This was precisely the path I hoped to follow one day. Amelia's courage, her ability to face the unknown, and her passion to seek justice resonated deeply with me. She was emotional, mind you—she teared up on multiple occasions—but that did not stop her from making all the right decisions. I struggled with this trait and hoped to achieve it someday—to not be cold-hearted and yet make intelligent decisions.

The movie strengthened my resolve to pursue my dreams, and it was my silent promise to Raha that we would stay on the right path. With each passing moment, our shared passion for the world of forensic science burned brighter, setting the stage for the extraordinary journey ahead.

My course was particularly stressful. It required a deep understanding of how DNA worked and how to meticulously screen for biological imprints at a crime scene to gather evidence. My first day of college was nothing short of a dream come true. I was introduced to a fascinating array of subjects, each holding unique promise and allure. Among them, the crime scene investigation lab stood out like a candy store. Pardon the analogy. It was challenging and demanded precision and attention to detail. But that's what made it so thrilling and attractive. After all, where's the fun if you get everything right on the first try?

As the years went by, the course explained the various methods of analyzing DNA, helping me master the art of delivering expert testimony for depositions. It was rigorous, testing my emotional as well as intelligence quotient (EQ and IQ) at every turn. But I welcomed every puzzle with open arms. The knowledge I gained in those classrooms and the practical experience I gathered during internships and fieldwork laid the foundation for my career.

However, my aspirations did not stop with forensic science. I wanted to understand the human mentality.

The question I wanted answered was, "Why do people commit crimes?"

The human psyche was genuinely mysterious. I wanted to understand the emotions and rationale (if any) behind every crime and the psychology and social factors that drove individuals to commit the unthinkable. Given a choice, shouldn't we all just do the right thing?

Was I being too idealistic? Or naive? I have often been called that. Often enough to wonder if it was a compliment or an insult.

College life not only opened the doors to a world of knowledge but also introduced me to some incredible fellow students who shared my passion. One of them was Niranjan, the son of a renowned criminologist. Through him, I had the privilege of meeting his mother, Mrs. Vaishnavi Balaji, who was like a superhero in the field of forensic science. Her fantastic work inspired me. Her determination and dedication were similar to Amelia's.

One of my favorite cases was nicknamed the 'Midnight Heist.' It was about a painting that was missing from the museum. The criminal had not only swapped the valuable painting with a convincing fake but had sold the original at an auction and was living a life of luxury. Mrs. Vaishnavi had examined the crime scene with her experienced eye, and while everyone else had focused on the obvious clues, she had observed something inconspicuous. It had been a tiny, almost invisible fiber caught on a hidden nail. This was no ordinary fiber; it was nearly invisible to the naked eye. She realized that it was an extremely rare thread used by artists who engaged in the black market. When examined under a special UV light, this thread showed a hidden pattern resembling the stolen art. The forger had a signature and had stolen numerous pieces from museums worldwide. That thread led the team to the thief.

I looked up all the cases and studied them every day. As my days turned into weeks and weeks into semesters, I sharpened my skills and made friends with similar minds. They loved solving mysteries just as much as I did, if not more. College life was proving to be incredible, filled with investigations, revelations, and the promise of a bright future in the world of forensic science and criminology.

CHAPTER FIVE

MY FIRST MYSTERY

Niranjan and I often headed to his house on weekends, where we shamelessly pestered his mother for details of her past cases. We would then conduct postmortem investigations and wonder about what we would have done had we been the lead on the case. During one such visit, she casually spoke about another case, which was an ongoing investigation.

The case revolved around smugglers who specialized in stealing and selling ivory and sandalwood, a crime that struck the heart of nature and the very forests that surrounded my home. These criminals operated under the cover of darkness, like phantoms of the forest, and were destroying the lush woods. Their greed for these prized resources posed a grave threat to the environment, wildlife, and the delicate balance of our ecosystem.

It's funny (in a non-funny way) how many do not realize the value of every animal and plant, as everything in nature is often in perfect balance. Humans are the only ones that disrupt it for instant gratification. If we really loved our children and cared about the upcoming generations, we would not behave this way.

This brings me back to the question: Why do we do what we do?

But let's get back to the case. As Mrs. Vaishnavi described the complexities of the investigation, I couldn't help being impressed by the details. The criminals were brilliant, too. I wondered why super-smart people were drawn to a life of crime. The world would be a much better place if this intelligence were put to good use.

Intelligence is not a privilege; it's a gift, and you should use it for the good of humanity. That's true, isn't it? If you have the ability to help someone, doesn't it become your responsibility to do so? This is certainly something to think about.

It was around this time that I spoke to her about my connection to the very crime she was investigating. I told her that my father had been tirelessly working to protect the same forests that these ruthless criminals were plundering. Neither of us had realized until then that such criminal activities were happening just a few kilometers away from our home.

The chase to put these smugglers behind bars was not just about solving a crime; it was a mission to safeguard the sanctity of our home and to shield it from those who sought to exploit it for their selfish gain. It was a battle to preserve the irreplaceable, to protect the voiceless animals of the woods, and to ensure that Kabini's beauty and wonder lasted for generations to come.

The line between my personal life and my passion for forensic science blurred, and a new, personal mission began. One that would take me deep into the heart of the forest, where I would confront not only criminals but also the mysteries of nature itself.

Then, the pandemic struck, disrupting life as we knew it. I mean, who would have thought that something created in one part of the world would affect everyone else? I have seen many zombie movies. But they were just morbid sci-fi theories. This had an impact on real life. My college shut down, and with travel ruled out, I found myself locked up at home. It was a challenging time for me. My parents, who were still required at work, were away as usual. The work-from-home concept did not apply to them, as their profession was such. I felt a growing sense of restlessness. Online classes, while informative, didn't provide the same sense of fulfillment that hands-on learning did. The spark I had once felt was missing.

Faced with this newfound uncertainty, I decided to take matters into my own hands. I resolved to work on the ivory and sandalwood smuggling case that had hit so close to home. When I shared my decision with my parents, they were surprisingly supportive. However, they had one non-negotiable condition—I could not venture into the forests pretending to be Amelia Donaghy. (I just nodded along. I mean, that was my mission. OK. My other mission).

With their blessings (sort of) and a commitment to follow their safety guidelines (mostly; Hey, I was not in a self-destructive mode), I began my journey of investigation and research. It was a new phase in my life, marked by challenges, self-discovery, and the pursuit of justice. Wow, that sentence has many big words! The pandemic might have halted many things, but it couldn't extinguish the fire of curiosity and passion that burned within me. All I needed was a cape and a mask to play the role. I was cool, yes, but I was yet to become cool enough to pull off that look. It was in the plan, though. A nice red cape, like a mix between Supergirl and the Incredibles. Hmmm. Skirt or pants, though?

Sorry, I am deviating from the narrative again. I really should get better at this.

I constantly stayed in touch with Niranjan. Our conversations continually went back to the case, and during one of these discussions, he dropped a bombshell. He had heard his mother talk about the smuggling being connected to a brown truck with the logo 'Manure For Nature' on it. Wasn't that smart? Who would stop a truck passing through the forest when it looked like it was out to save the environment? Come to think of it, almost all villains are ingenious. If they used their brains and skills for good, they could work towards saving the planet.

Let's get back to the story.

According to an eyewitness, this truck was spotted just outside the forests in Karnataka, but its presence was yet to be officially verified.

I forgot to tell you. We had another duty added to our crime-solving case—spying and getting clues from our respective parents. Clearly, we did not respect their privacy. All covert operations are like that. And our intentions were good. So, it's all right. That's right! We decide that. We don't have X-ray vision and super hearing. This is all we've got, isn't it? So we must snoop and overhear.

That did sound bad. So, we also swore to work on stealth investigative strategies that would be acceptable to the jury. (By the way, does India decide court cases via a jury?) Anyway, let's use the word 'observe' and not 'stalk' for the sake of this story, shall we? We are the good guys, after all! Let's do it right.

The information about the truck was unverified. It was not much, but it was enough to qualify as the breakthrough we had been waiting for. It was a breadcrumb and a sliver of hope. Amelia had had a lot less when she was trying to solve a crime. That helped me convince myself.

CAN I SOLVE IT?

Around a week later, as the sun dipped below the horizon, my attention was drawn to a brown truck as it passed right by my house. The vehicle was battery-operated and was probably used to move stealthily. I was sure that it was a clever tactic employed by the smugglers to evade detection. I almost missed it. The excessive hooting of an owl called out to me. I picked up the phone immediately to inform Niranjan about it. He told me to hold my horses and that following the truck was not a smart move. He said he would speak to his mother and get back to me. We were asking for trouble because we were not supposed to know about the truck. He had to present his case in such a way that we would not get grounded. So, all I had to do was sit next to the phone and stay calm, without alarming my parents.

Yeah right. Me and stay calm. I was anything but calm, even on a normal day. Now, I was just beyond hyper.

My growing concern turned into sheer panic when my father failed to return home that night. My mother, though worried, managed to hold herself together. It didn't take a forensic scientist to connect the dots. Something was wrong, and I knew I had to do something. Calling Niranjan was a lost cause. So, I did what I did best. Be impulsive and do what my gut told me to.

As I wished my mother goodnight, I reassured her that all would be well the next day. However, my words sounded hollow to my ears. I decided to take matters into my own hands. With a sense of urgency coursing through me, I carefully gathered my forensic kit, ensuring that I had everything I might need:

- Two flashlights (there is no such thing as too many of those)

- Extra batteries (same logic)

- A forensic light source (a tool used by detectives and forensic investigators to reveal and analyze trace evidence that is not easily visible under normal lighting conditions)

- A digital camera (not cool to use a smartphone if I plan to become a serious detective, yes?)

- A magnifying glass and a pair of night-vision binoculars

- Latex gloves and paper shoe covers

Yup, my bag was not a small one. I also took protein bars and water. I needed a lot of energy.

It was pitch dark now. My heart was pounding, and I was terrified. This was not a fun mission. My father could be in trouble. I could not sit back and do nothing. Would Amelia sit at home? Nope. In hindsight, maybe I should have called the cops or something. But hey, hindsight is always 20/20. Anyway, I am not going to ruin your next chapter.

As I wandered into the forest, walking down the path I had taken countless times during my leisurely strolls, I knew I wasn't alone. That kept me going. Raha was by my side the whole time, though her presence carried an unusual weight. She was unhappy about this one-man show. Sorry, a one-woman show. Actually, it was a two-woman show. Just because she was invisible doesn't mean I cannot count her presence, yes? The crusade to find my father amidst her disapproval was weighing me down. Her usual chatter was absent, and she refused to engage with me because I had ignored her warning. Yet, she remained steadfast, walking beside me in silent protest. It was like she wanted to tell me something but couldn't. Like she knew what was going to happen but was bound by an unwritten clause to stay silent.

As we went deeper into the forest, I noticed an abnormal amount of dirt piled on the left side of the trail. It was arranged in a straight line. It seemed like a sneaky attempt to conceal the tracks of a vehicle, likely the same battery-operated truck I had spotted near my house. I couldn't ignore this obvious sign. The universe was giving me a sign. And I followed.

I was a third-year student in the field of forensic science, and such details did not escape my eye. I followed the concealed trail for another kilometer until I saw a very ordinary-looking shed. So ordinary, I could have ignored it.

My instincts screamed. I wanted to turn and run, to seek help and make sure nothing terrible happened to me. But Amelia's voice pushed me not to give up. I wanted to find my dad and put the bad guys behind bars. I wanted to get home safe and sound. The list was endless.

I inched closer to the shed. The bag on my back was getting heavier by the second. Above the entrance to the shed, a sign read, 'Forest Range Store Room.' The name was not unfamiliar to me. I had read about forest management and wildlife protection. My father had told me about it as well. This was not a frequently used space; it was only needed in an SOS scenario.

The room was no ordinary storage space; it was designed to safeguard valuable items against fire and theft. What secrets did it hold? Would I find the answers I so desperately sought within its crumbling walls? There was no turning back now, and with a deep breath, I reached for the door handle, ready to face whatever lay inside.

CHAPTER SEVEN

POINT OF NO RETURN

I pushed the door wide open, and the room seemed to call out to me. The wide range of tools and gear was well beyond a basic survival kit. Each item was designed for a range of activities, from collecting evidence to drawing conclusions.

I picked out what I needed. It wasn't hard. A first-aid kit, a thermal imaging camera to measure heat profiles of the surroundings, a thematic map, and a flare gun. I hoped that I wouldn't need the flare gun. I left the walkie-talkie behind. Who would I speak to?

As I scanned the bookshelf, my eyes landed on a book that I had always yearned to read. However, my excitement was reduced when I realized that it refused to budge from its snug spot. I tugged at it repeatedly, only to discover that it was not really a book. It was a handle. A rush of cool air brushed against my hand, confirming that this was the key to something weird.

As I stood there, wishing it was a secret door, a voice boomed beside me. "Go home. Get help. You are not supposed to be here."

I had forgotten about Raha. Her voice made me jump out of my skin. I almost screamed. For the first time in my life, I had forgotten about her. She was not wrong, though. But then, neither was I. I had to save my dad. Her (now annoying) whispers of caution tugged at my conscience, but I couldn't shake the image of my dad tied up somewhere, his fate unknown. My fingers danced over the books, searching for the button that would swing open the bookshelf.

Among the books, one stood out, not because of its title, but because it had a small, gorgeously designed butterfly perched on its spine. It looked out of place, like a puzzle piece that didn't quite fit. I pressed the butterfly gently, and to my amazement, the bookshelf shivered as if waking from a deep slumber. It moved slowly but steadily. Surprisingly, it did not make any noise. Not a creak. Like it was well-oiled and used regularly.

The door revealed a hidden passage. A rush of cool, forest-scented air greeted me. I don't know how that happened and there were no windows.

Despite my resolution to proceed, Raha's whispered words of caution tugged at my conscience.

Her voice, a blend of concern and fear, echoed in my mind. "Don't get into trouble. Go and call for help."

For a moment, I hesitated, torn between my longing to find my dad and her sensible advice. But the urgency of the situation made me ignore her. With a determined shake of my head, I decided to proceed, but not without a plan in mind. I would explore cautiously, staying vigilant for any sign of danger, and if needed, I would call for help at the first sign of trouble. I stepped into the hidden passage, ready to face whatever lay ahead.

"Get help. Now. Go back. You are not supposed to be here. It will be too late."

I kept walking.

CHAPTER EIGHT

WHAT LIES BENEATH

The passage was dark, long, and scary. As I walked further into it, I encountered a steep, winding staircase that seemed to descend endlessly into the earth. The steps were uneven and worn out. I had to watch my step. If I fell, there wouldn't be anyone to help me.

As I cautiously made my way down, my flashlight cast scary shadows, highlighting the hidden world beneath the forest floor. Suddenly, I found myself face-to-face with a pack of curious rats, their tiny eyes glinting in the dim light. I froze, momentarily startled. But they quickly hurried away as if they were granting me passage. Or they were just as scared of me as I was of them. Either way, I was free to proceed.

Further along, I encountered a colony of bats hanging upside down from the ceiling like natural chandeliers. Their wings rustled softly, sending shivers down my spine, but I pressed on. I didn't cringe or scream. Besides, they were ignoring me. I didn't matter to them. They probably knew I was harmless. Or rather, I couldn't harm them even if I wanted to.

The passageway took another turn, and there, coiled and ready to strike, was a small rattlesnake. It hissed, its rattle signifying a warning. Now, I knew I couldn't afford to get bitten, so I carefully backed away, my heart pounding. There is a very fine line between stupidity and bravery, and this rattlesnake was that line.

I took another route, hoping that I was not losing my way any more than earlier. But are you lost if you do not know where you are going? Something to think about! As I descended the steep, winding steps and plunged into the depths of the passage, my heart raced with excitement and fear. The earth beneath the forest was ready to scream her secrets out, and I was sure that I was on the verge of an incredible discovery.

I reached the end of the passage, where a massive door stood before me. It had a mysterious keypad and was locked by a passcode. As I pondered over it, I noticed something remarkable. There was a series of symbols etched on the doorframe, each corresponding to a specific button on the keypad.

With a mix of excitement and intuition, I realized that these symbols were clues, a secret code that nature herself had created. They represented the elements of the forest and consisted of imprints of leaves, animals, and patterns on the bark of trees. It was the Fibonacci sequence. I had just watched the Da Vinci Code for the nth time, and the answer was obvious to me.

This is how it worked. The sequence followed the rule that each number equals the sum of the preceding two numbers. It was a simple addition puzzle. But you must identify the pattern correctly. I carefully pressed the buttons in the sequence of symbols, and to my amazement, the door creaked open, granting me entry into the heart of the smuggler's hidden lair.

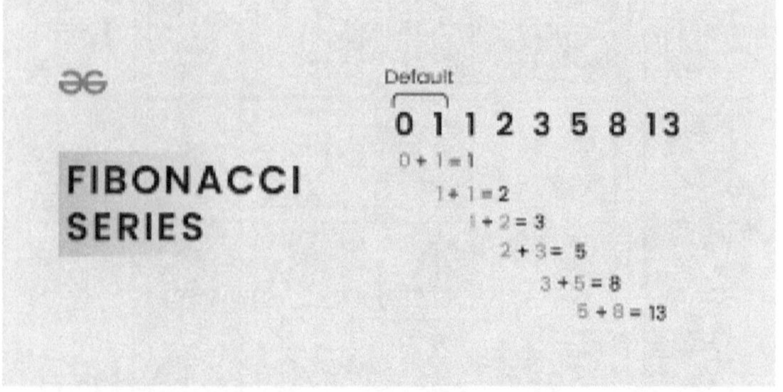

Raha stopped talking to me. I wasn't complaining. She was not letting me solve this mystery. I was glad she kept her negative thoughts to herself. Under any other circumstances, her uncharacteristic silence might have irritated me. But not now. I was completely consumed by the excitement, nervousness, and fear that coursed through my veins (I wonder why it wasn't the arteries). The investigation had captured my attention fully, and my invisible friend's silence had become a mere backdrop to the drama happening before me.

As I stepped through the massive door at the end of the hidden passage, I found myself in a room. I froze. The atmosphere was filled with a bone-chilling cold that seemed to freeze my very soul. The eerie silence that enveloped the room was so palpable that it echoed in my ears.

The space in front of me was vast, far larger, and more spacious than I could have ever imagined. It seemed to stretch endlessly. It was as if nature herself had carved out this hidden sanctuary.

Ivory and sandalwood piles stood tall, displaying the illegal trade's exploitation of precious resources. The ivory gleamed with an otherworldly, ghostly beauty, the striking white tusks standing in stark contrast to the shadows surrounding them. The sandalwood logs lay in orderly rows, their scent hanging heavily in the air, a haunting reminder of the trees that had been felled for profit.

It was a place where secrets were buried, and that is where I now stood. I was determined to uncover the truth and end the crimes that affected all of us. I could have turned around at this point. But I had to prove my point. Raha was ignoring me. And I ignored her. Two can play the game.

Yes, I was upset with her. This was the time I needed her the most. But she chose to be quiet. Hence, my reaction.

CHAPTER NINE

WHAT LAY AHEAD

In the dimly lit corner of the oversized room, I noticed a small door. It seemed very out of place. I listened carefully, telling myself to keep quiet. Soft sounds that felt like the clanging of metal, like handcuffs tapping against the table, reached my ears. A chilling realization washed over me, and I felt like I had been drenched in icy water. I had a sinking feeling as I guessed what lay ahead.

My heart raced, and for a moment, I contemplated running away as fast as my legs would carry me. I wished I had sought help when the opportunity presented itself instead of relying on my amateurish knowledge and youthful enthusiasm.

It was too late for sanity and logic to kick in. I had already jumped into the proverbial troubled waters. It was now time to swim and not contemplate heading back to the shore. With trembling hands, I pushed open the door to the dingy room, and there, in the flickering light, I saw my dad. His eyes widened as if he had seen a ghost. I realized that he was no longer scared for his own life. He was afraid for me. The scene in the room told me everything.

My whole body went cold. I had never felt fear like that, not even when I saw a bear running across the road or a baby leopard whizz past my tree house.

A sharp pang of pain shot through my head. The world around me became a blur, and I felt dizzy. Before I could comprehend what was happening, the darkness swallowed me. I blacked out, my consciousness slipping away like a whisper in the wind.

Several minutes or hours had passed since then. I couldn't tell. I awoke to a disorienting reality. My hands were bound firmly behind my back, leaving me feeling utterly helpless. My father was missing, and the room was filled with a strange stillness that was suffocating. But what was most unsettling was Raha's absence. She wasn't just silent; she was not here with me anymore.

I began to panic and called out to her. But there was no response. She had been a constant presence in my life, accompanying me through every experience. Now, in this dire moment of need, she had simply vanished.

All the moments I had shared with Raha flashed before my eyes. How I had always felt at ease with her. How we were so alike. As I gazed at the door that stayed shut, it suddenly hit me. HARD. Raha. She wasn't a figment of my imagination. I realized why she had seemed so familiar to me all along. She liked the same things I did. Reacted to situations just like I did. We got along like we were sisters and had the same thoughts.

Because we were the same! Raha was me from the future. I had come back to the past to prevent myself from reaching this very moment in time. But she was not here now.

Several questions boggled my mind, each stranger than the last, as I struggled to understand what was happening. If Raha had gone missing, what did it mean for me? Would my life end here, in this cold, dark room?

Did I even have a future?

PART II

AGNI:
THE SUPERHERO

PROLOGUE

There comes a time when it does not matter what other people think because, deep down, you are sure of who you are.

There are times when you should stand up for yourself—your rights, your place in society—and for those who cannot stand up for themselves.

This is what Agni, our superhero, signifies. She knows all about your rights. But, she does not grant them easily. She wants to make sure that you do your fair share of work, i.e., your duties. It's a give-and-take policy, my friend.

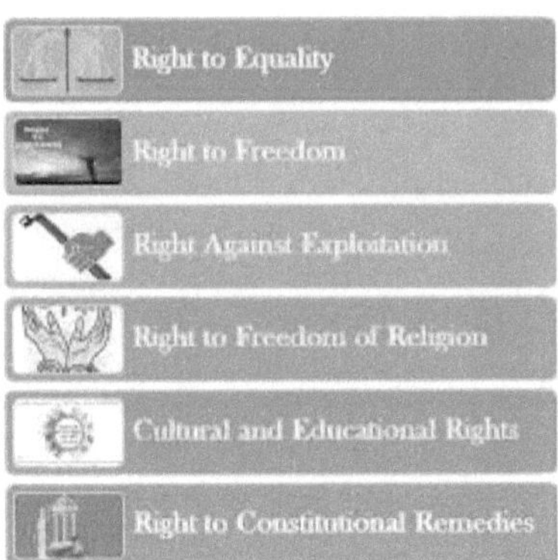

Fundamental Duties of Indian Citizens

To abide by the Constitution and respect its ideals and institutions, the National Flag and the National Anthem

To cherish and follow the noble ideals which inspired our national struggle for freedom

To uphold and protect the sovereignty, unity and integrity of India;

To defend the country and render national service when called upon to do so

To promote harmony and the spirit of common brotherhood amongst all the people of India transcending religious, linguistic and regional or sectional diversities; to renounce practices derogatory to the dignity of women

To value and preserve the rich heritage of our composite culture

To protect and improve the natural environment including forests, lakes, rivers and wildlife and to have compassion for living creatures

To develop the scientific temper, humanism and the spirit of inquiry and reform

To safeguard public property and to abjure violence

To strive towards excellence in all spheres of individual and collective activity so that the nation constantly rises to higher levels of endeavour and achievement

Hey, Young Minds of India!

You are the heart and soul of this incredible nation, and I am sure you are filled with dreams and fantasies. Before we go into the story of the superhero who made it her mission to fight for the rights of those around her, I would like to leave you with a message. Let's talk about what really matters to you and the future you dream for your country.

Let's say that I give you a magical bag of marbles. Each marble represents a day of your life. You start with a full bag, but you take out one marble every day. When all the marbles are gone, so is your time.

Here's the thing: the magic is not in having the most marbles but in what you do with them. Each day is special because it doesn't last forever.

So, what do you do with your marbles? Do you spend them wisely, doing things that matter to you? You may use one marble to learn a new skill, another to help a friend, and yet another to explore a new place. Each marble you use adds to the story of your life.

What are your priorities? Please write them down before you proceed.

There will be sunny days when everything feels perfect and rainy days when you feel lost and alone. But, even on those dark days, you can hold onto hope like a bright light, and it will point you in the right direction.

Remember, you're stronger than any challenge you face. You can turn your struggles into strengths like a caterpillar that turns into a butterfly. So, make your life meaningful. Fight for what you believe in, irrespective of the obstacles you face.

My dear friend, make each day count as you journey through life. Be brave, be kind, and most importantly, be true to yourself. And even if you stumble along the way, know that living with purpose brings joy.

Today, I say this to remind you that time is a gift. Don't waste it living someone else's life. Make yours count. Fight for what you hold dear because even if you fall short, living authentically is the greatest achievement of all.

Young India, you have the power to shape the future. Let's work together to build the India of your dreams —a nation of prosperity, inclusivity, and limitless possibilities. Together, you will carry each other into the future.

CHAPTER ONE

FUNDAMENTAL RIGHTS, DUTIES, AND YOU

Everyone makes a big deal about rights. And rightly so (pun intended). As a citizen of India, you are born with the power to live freely, speak your mind, and choose your path. But with great power comes great responsibility. Uncle Ben was a genius, wasn't he? And, of course, so was Stan Lee.

It's not just about what you can do; it's also about what you should do. Your rights are like superpowers, and how you use them truly defines you. And then comes the other side of the coin—your duties. What are they? Rights are what we expect others to do for us, while duties are the actions we should take for others. Therefore, having a right also means having an obligation to respect the rights of others. These obligations, which are linked to rights, manifest as duties.

Let me explain with an example. I would ideally like to talk about the environment, but I will start small. Take your room—or the room you share with your sibling. You have the right to a clean room, yes? It should be hygienic, filled with clean air, well-organized, and produce a good vibe so that you can invite your friends over without cringing.

So, how would that happen? This right comes with a corresponding responsibility, and this is where you come in again. You have the duty to clean your room and not litter it. You must put things back in their proper places. By fulfilling your duty, you not only protect your own right to a clean environment but also ensure that anyone who uses the room can appreciate it for the right reasons.

Here's a trick question for you. Is doing your homework your right or your duty?

I'll answer that for you.

Doing homework can be seen as both a right and a duty, depending on the perspective. You have the right to education, which includes the responsibility to complete assigned tasks to learn and grow. It's also a duty because completing homework helps you develop essential skills like responsibility, time management, and perseverance, which are valuable for your future.

Remember. Nothing is more expensive than a missed opportunity. Do your bit. Leave the rest to what comes along.

Bhagavad Gita, Chapter 2, Verse 47 says:

कर्मण्येवाधिकारस्ते मा फलेषु कदाचन।

मा कर्मफलहेतुर्भूर्मा ते सङ्गोऽस्त्वकर्मणि॥ २-४७

Karmanye vadhikaraste Ma Phaleshu Kadachana,

Ma Karmaphalaheturbhurma Te Sangostvakarmani

This verse means:

You have the right to the work alone but never to its fruits.

Let not the fruits of action be your motive, nor let your attachment be to inaction.

As a student, you might feel that if you have studied for five hours daily, you deserve full marks on the tests. Does life really work like that? If only that were true. Life often has its own way of testing us, and success is not always directly proportional to our efforts. Sometimes, factors beyond our control or unforeseen circumstances can influence the outcome. So, while hard work is essential and can increase your chances of success, it's also important to be prepared for life's unpredictability.

Sometimes, even if you study really hard, you might not get top marks. Life can often be like a game where the rules change suddenly. For example, you might prepare a lot for a test, but the questions could differ from what you expected. Or you might practice a speech very well. You might have stood in front of the mirror or your family and friends and would have pulled it off very well. But then, when D-day arrives, you feel nervous when speaking in front of strangers. You often do not see that coming. It certainly does not demean the efforts you have invested, but they do not guarantee results.

These moments show us that while working hard is important, being able to adjust to changes and not giving up when things get tough are also very necessary. So, it's good to work hard but also be ready for unexpected challenges along the way. That is why the quote from the Bhagavad Gita can be a life-changer.

Just do your best. Give it your all, no matter how trivial the task or challenge. It might seem impossible.

"How can I not expect something?" you may ask.

Trust me, the best of us struggle with this. But in the end, it might actually be liberating. You free yourself from unnecessary stress and open yourself to new possibilities and opportunities for growth.

So, without further ado, let's step into the world of our superhero.

CHAPTER TWO

SAKTHI

Meet Sakthi, a girl from the small town of Kumbakonam, Tamil Nadu. She isn't your typical 23-year-old. She holds a postgraduate degree in Human Rights and Duties from Madras University, because why not? But that isn't all. She has a knack for writing too. She's even taken journalism and creative writing courses. Sakthi works in a bank during the first half of the day and as a freelance reporter for the local newspaper during her free time. She's a girl who has her cake and eats it, too. She is keen on making a difference without changing who she is.

How does she do it all? Because she believes that it is a mistake to think that you know everything. It prevents you from learning. So she studies whenever possible.

Right to Equality & Vote
Respect the constitution & National Symbols
Right to Freedom of Speech and Expression
Uphold & Protect the Sovereignty, Unity & Integrity of India
Right to Education and Basic Necessities
Protect the Environment & Have Compassion for Living Creatures
Right to Freedom of Religion & Conscience
Defend the Country & Render National Service
Right to Constitutional Remedies
Ensure Value Education to strive for Excellence & National Growth
Rights
Duties

Now, what makes Sakthi truly special is that her personality is a rare mix of fun and seriousness. At 23, she's as lively and bubbly as a five-year-old chasing bubbles in the park. Yet, when it comes to life's complexities, she's as sharp as a 45-year-old solving the cryptex. You should look up this puzzle when you can.

Trivia time

The cryptex operates like a combination lock on a bicycle. By aligning the dials correctly, the lock can be opened. The most common cryptex is equipped with five lettered dials. There are five turntables on the cipher cylinder, each with 26 letters. There are 11,881,376 possible permutations. When these dials are rotated to form the correct sequence, the tumblers inside align themselves and allow the cylinder to slide apart. Within the cryptex lies a glass vial filled with vinegar. If the cryptex were to break open, the vial would shatter, and the vinegar would dissolve the secret written in the papyrus placed within, effectively destroying it.

The cryptex is a fictional vault that appears in Dan Brown's 2003 novel The Da Vinci Code. However, a real cryptex was created in 2004 by Justin Kirk Nevins.

Why did we read about the cryptex? Because it's nice to know about things. ☺

Now, let's get back to the story.

Sakthi is a spark that can brighten a room faster than you can say 'cheese.' Her smile has a twinkle that can outshine the stars, and her zest for life is downright contagious.

Now, Sakthi's childhood wasn't any different from the rest of us. But here's how she was special—she had a knack for making lemonade out of lemons. Yep, when life threw curveballs at her, she turned them into fun-flavored candies.

Her Pollyanna spirit wasn't just about saying 'thank you' to life; she was truly grateful and appreciative in every way. She didn't accept life as a formality; she wrapped her arms around it and gave it a bear hug.

Trivia time for Pollyanna

The book Pollyanna is about an optimistic young girl who, after being orphaned, goes to live with her grumpy aunt and transforms the town with her positive attitude. Because of its popularity, 'Pollyanna' is now a term used to describe someone who, like the character, is always optimistic. This positive bias is known as the Pollyanna principle.

Sakthi's part-time workplace, the small online and offline newspaper, was connected with just about everyone, from naughty little ones to wise old owls. It was like a one-stop shop for news. The paper had a separate fun section for kids, while the section for grown-ups had all the serious stuff that would make you nod like a learned sage.

But here's the kicker—the articles didn't gossip about celebs or discuss fashion trends. Nope, they were all about real news, news that matters. The kind that made you say, 'Hey, I didn't know that!' and, 'I should do something about it!' The articles gave the audience information that made a difference and spoke about truths that had to be told.

To give you an example, Sakthi's latest article was about a local charity organization that was struggling to provide meals for homeless people. The content highlighted their efforts and the urgent need for support. The article had a deep impact, and both children and adults were inspired to act and do something about it. Children organized bake sales, lemonade stands, and donation drives at their schools and neighborhoods. Adults joined in by organizing charity events, fundraising campaigns, and spreading awareness on social media. Together, they collected substantial funds and resources for the NGO so that it could continue providing meals. The community's response demonstrated the power of information to mobilize people and make a meaningful difference in the lives of others.

At the end of the day, there should be a takeaway from any content you read. Do you agree? Sakthi wrote to create change, to change the world, to bring quality to life, and to protect everyone's rights and duties to live their lives with dignity, equality, and respect.

This world was Sakthi's stage, where her serious drive, ambitious spirit, and caring nature defined everything in her life. She was passionate about her job. It wasn't just work; it was her way of making the world a tad brighter. She knew that her career had the power to make readers think and act. So the responsibility of being accurate, critical, and fair was on her.

Her favorite topic of discussion was an area where she was an expert—human rights and duties. It might sound like boring grown-up stuff, but it's not. All of us should know about them and take the right action. Such issues especially mattered to her because they held the secrets to making communities a whole lot better. Think about it. If everyone had access to clean water, good health, education, employment, and a safe environment, wouldn't India be on its way to becoming a developed country?

There is a reason Civics is taught in schools at a young age. Yes, it is important to become doctors, engineers, and high-profile professionals. But it is just as awesome to become a game changer by taking charge of the nation. And this begins with taking care of its citizens and residents.

To be a rock star citizen or a community champion, you've got to understand your rights and your duties. This was crystal clear to her, yet Sakthi couldn't understand why others could not see it. To her, it was the same as explaining why ice cream is delicious on a hot summer day—it was a no-brainer!

So, what are these rights? Let's take a look.

Right	Explanation
Right to Equality	This means that everyone should be treated equally before the law. No one should be discriminated against based on factors like caste, gender, religion, or place of birth. In simple terms, everyone's got a fair shot!
Right to Freedom	This is about freedom of speech, expression, assembly, and more. You have the right to say what's on your mind (within limits, of course) and move about as you please. It's like the world's your oyster!
Right Against Exploitation	Nobody should be mistreated or forced to work against their will. For example, no one can force you to do their homework, even if they offer candy.
Right to Freedom of Religion	You can practice and preach your religion freely. You're free to follow your faith, religion, or spirituality.
Cultural and Educational Rights	These rights protect your culture, language, and access to education. You've got the right to celebrate your traditions and hit the books.
Right to Constitutional Remedies	This is your superpower to go to court if your rights are violated. It's like having a direct hotline to a superhero lawyer when things go wrong.

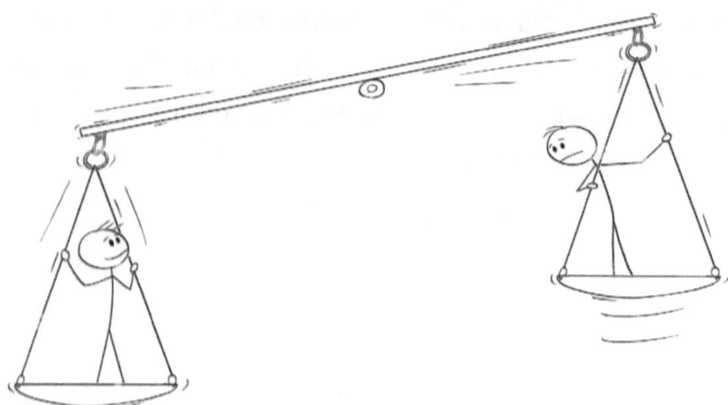

But with these rights come duties as well. This is a give-and-take policy, isn't it?

Fundamental duty	Explanation
Respect the Constitution	It's like following the rules of your clubhouse, but this one's called the Constitution. You respect its laws, values, and national symbols like the Flag and Anthem.
Uphold National Ideals	Imagine being inspired by the stories of your grandparents and their fight for freedom. That's what this duty is all about—carrying forward the noble ideals of our national struggle.
Protect Sovereignty	Just like we would protect our treehouse from outsiders, we must safeguard our country's unity and integrity. It's a bit like being a guardian of our nation's secrets.
Defend and Serve the Nation	Sometimes, when our nation needs help, we've got to answer its call. It's like signing up for superhero duty when our country needs a hand.
Promote Unity and Harmony	Being nice to everyone, no matter where they're from or what language they speak. It is like sharing your toys with everyone.
Preserve Cultural Heritage	Think of it as taking care of your grandma's old recipes—it's about preserving our rich cultural traditions.
Protect the Environment	Protecting the environment is like keeping your backyard clean and your pet goldfish happy. It's about showing some love and care to Mother Nature.
Embrace Science	It means having boundless curiosity that makes you question things for continuous learning. Put in the effort to ensure the world becomes a better place through science and reason. Yes, it's okay to ask questions. Even about the necessity of consuming green vegetables. But do not be a rebel for the sake of being one.

Fundamental duty	Explanation
Safeguard Public Property	Don't break or damage public property. Maintain your community's infrastructure and peace.
Strive for Excellence	Just like you do your best to improve your score in your favorite video game, do your best in everything for the country's benefit.
Ensure Children are Educated	If you're a parent or a guardian, you will ensure your children attend school. It's all about giving kids the opportunity to learn. If you are a student, make sure you study. And study well. Your future and the future of your country depend on it.

And don't forget to vote. There's no point in just sitting at home and whining about things that are not right. Do something about it. Vote. Pay your taxes on time. Spare time for social work. Stand for elections. Join the team that makes things happen, not the one that just watches.

Martha Gellhorn said, "People often proudly say, 'I'm not interested in politics.' They might as well say, 'I'm not interested in my standard of living, my health, my job, my rights, my freedom, my future, or any future.' If we want to keep any control over our world and our lives, we must be interested in politics."

Your voice matters, and your actions can shape the future you want to see.

So, step up, get involved, and make a difference.

Remember, if you avoid conflict to keep the peace, you start a war inside yourself.

(Please read this line again).

WINNING THE TRIP

Now that we've nailed the basics, it is time to buckle up for the ride. Let us dive into Sakthi's adventure and discover how she became a superhero! Believe it or not, it's a transformation that's mind-blowing. So get ready for some serious awesomeness! The earlier chapter just introduced her and told you what she believed in, but there's so much more to come. Don't get me wrong; she was already amazing. She knew the difference between right and wrong. She didn't just write about it; she took action.

Let me give you an example.

Back when she was in primary school, Sakthi got wind of a problem. A girl named Riya, who lived in her neighborhood, was mistreated. She had a physical disability, and a gang of children made fun of her. Now, that is not right at all. Anyone would be affected by this kind of behavior. And Riya was a sensitive child. This ill-treatment pushed her over the edge. She stopped going to school. Sakthi stepped up. With the family's permission, she wrote an emotional yet accurate piece bringing awareness to the issue (without taking any names, of course) while sensitizing the school and the parents to the issue. Knowing she had all the support she needed, Riya returned to school. The bullies were afraid to go anywhere near her because they knew they would be watched.

That is the power of the written word. It might seem like all talk, but somehow, somewhere, it registers in the minds of people and makes an impact when it matters.

That's Sakthi for you, our everyday superhero, turning wrong into right and making the world a better place, one clever move at a time. When she became a superhero, she became super awesome. Let's go back in time to how she became super. She developed some pretty cool abilities and could do things that you and I could only dream about.

When Sakthi completed Class 11, she participated in a group competition conducted by her school. The objective of the competition was to stimulate creativity and encourage participants to devise practical solutions for real-world problems.

Living in South India, the most obvious problem she wanted to solve was accessibility to clean and potable water. This project was a good idea because it addressed a critical issue. Access to safe drinking water is a significant challenge in many parts of South

India, leading to various health issues and hardships for communities. By focusing on this problem, the project had the potential to improve the quality of life for many people, ensuring better health and well-being. Addressing water accessibility also aligned with broader sustainability goals, as clean water is essential for human survival and environmental health.

The idea was to have a device at home to grade and purify the water before consuming it. This device would be economically feasible and easy to maintain without requiring batteries.

Summary of the project

- **Device:** Solar-powered water purifier

- **Problem statement:** Access to clean and safe drinking water is a crucial challenge for many low-income families, particularly in areas with unreliable or contaminated water sources.

- **Solution:** The device comprised a portable water purifier with a solar panel.

- **About the portable water purifier:** The device included a compact and easily transportable water purifier capable of filtering and purifying water from various sources, such as rivers, ponds, or wells. It used a combination of advanced filtration methods to remove impurities and pathogens.

- **Solar panel:** A small solar panel was integrated into the device. It harnessed solar energy to power the purification process. This not only made the device energy-efficient but also eliminated the need for a constant power supply, which could be unreliable in low-income areas.

Features and benefits:

- Portable and compact design for easy transportation

- Advanced filtration methods to remove impurities and pathogens

- Solar panel for energy-efficient operation

- Suitable for purifying water from rivers, ponds, or wells

- Provides access to clean and safe drinking water, addressing a crucial need for low-income families

- Helps reduce the risk of waterborne diseases, improving overall health and well-being

How to use:

- Place the device in direct sunlight to charge the solar panel

- Fill the water purifier with water from a river, pond, or well

- Turn the purifier on and allow the water to pass through the filtration system

- Collect the purified water for consumption or storage

- Note the pH, chlorine, and heavy metal numbers before and after purification for reference

The final step was to monitor the effectiveness of the purification process and ensure that the water was safe to drink.

A committee of experts from various fields, including engineering, environmental science, public health, social work, and sustainable development, evaluated and validated the project. This multidisciplinary approach ensured the project was thoroughly examined from different perspectives, ensuring its feasibility, effectiveness, and potential impact.

The committee reviewed the project's documentation, including its design, technology, and proposed implementation strategy. They also spoke with the project team to understand their vision, approach, and commitment. The session ended after a viva (oral examination) was conducted. The team presented their project in detail, answered questions, and defended their ideas and methodologies.

After careful evaluation, the committee determined that the solar-powered water purifier project was innovative, technically sound, and would potentially be able to address the critical issue of access to clean water in low-income communities. As a result, it was selected as the winner among hundreds of submissions nationwide, highlighting its excellence and potential for positive impact.

Start-ups began making offers to bring this device to life, showing their readiness to take it to the next level. Team Sakthi won a trip to the Andaman Islands for their proof of concept.

CHAPTER FOUR

THE TRIP

Andaman Islands adventure itinerary

Island trivia

The Andaman Islands are a group of islands in the Bay of Bengal known for their stunning natural beauty and rich biodiversity. They are home to indigenous tribes, pristine beaches, and lush tropical forests. The islands are popular tourist destinations, offering opportunities for snorkeling, diving, and exploring vibrant marine life. The islands also have a rich history, with remnants of colonial-era structures along with a dark past as a former penal colony, the Ross Island Penal Colony.

A penal colony is a settlement used to exile prisoners and separate them from the general population. These colonies are often located in remote or distant areas and are used as a form of punishment or rehabilitation. Historically, various countries have used penal colonies to manage their prison populations and deter crime.

Despite their remote location, the Andaman Islands are easily accessible by air and sea, making them a must-visit destination for nature lovers and adventure seekers. The students were very excited. They ensured that they looked up all the places they were going to visit and decided on what they could do. How often does one get a chance like this, and at that age?

This was their itinerary.

Day 1 - Arrival

Catch the morning flight to the Andaman Islands, a real-life Nemo's paradise.

Set up camp in Port Blair.

Day 2 - Uncover history

Dive into the past at the iconic Cellular Jail, where our freedom fighters wrote their heroic stories.

Feel the echoes of their bravery in every cell.

Day 3 - Ross Island Odyssey

Time to island-hop! Ross Island is home to an array of wildlife.

You can see monkeys swing from vines and peacocks flaunt their feathers.

Day 4 - Ocean's Bounty

Ready to meet the underwater locals? Snorkeling time! Swim with the fishes, explore coral reefs, and maybe even find Nemo!

Day 5 - Culture and sunsets

Discover the island's rich culture at the Anthropological Museum.

Enjoy the spectacular view at Chidiya Tapu and watch the sun set into the ocean.

Day 6 – Bid adieu

It's the last hurrah in Nemo's kingdom.

Board the return flight home with tons of pictures and memories.

The school's idea while arranging this trip was to help students explore and experience independence during this excursion. They could break away from the crowd and travel solo on their Andaman adventure. Students were allowed to travel independently and get a taste of living and exploring the islands on their own terms. The offer was like a backstage pass to freedom—a ticket to discover the world and themselves. The journey was their book, and every step was a page they wrote on their own. It was wild, it was true, and it was like being an adult on a trial basis. Of course, there were a few conditions. They had to give status updates thrice a day, and their phones were geo-tagged the whole time.

The students had one more assignment. Every night, before going to bed, they had to create a vlog—a video log in which they narrated what happened during the day, their emotions and thoughts, and their takeaway from the experience.

Sakthi knew that her trip to the Andamans would be brilliant. When she landed on Havelock, an enchanting island nearly 100 kilometers from the mainland, her heart did a little happy dance.

With a sense of daring, she decided to rent a motorboat and was determined to cross the vast, open ocean all on her own. She packed enough food to keep her going for five days, even though she thought she'd be back in three. It was a once-in-a-lifetime opportunity. She wanted to make sure she had the energy for it.

She stumbled upon a beautiful, quiet island and decided to hang out there for a while. She swam in the ocean, built sandcastles, and stir-fried some vegetables. They tasted just a touch terrible, but she was proud of herself. What really caught her fancy was the sunset. She planned to watch it every evening. She'd plop down on the beach and watch the sun go down every single day. She would eat some food and just chill without any exam tension, responsibilities, or deadlines. Just her, doing nothing. It is funny that many people think you are productive only when there is a tangible output. That's not true. Sometimes, just taking that time off and focusing on... well... nothing, can also amount to something.

Sakthi's adventure stepped up a notch when she signed up for scuba diving. Diving at Nemo Reef on Havelock Island was a popular and rewarding experience. The reef was named after the abundant clownfish found there. She booked her dive online with Experience Yourselves. She appreciated the government's efforts and the 20% discount (thanks to her school). The dive site exceeded her expectations, with clear weather and calm waters. The sun beat down on her as the dive boat rocked gently back and forth. Sakthi was now far away from the shore. She could barely see the land. A shiver of excitement ran through her as she prepared to take the plunge. She had always dreamed of exploring the underwater world, and now, with the help of a seasoned diving expert, her dream was about to become a reality.

After receiving a quick tutorial on the diving equipment and proper breathing techniques from her instructor, Sakthi slipped into her wetsuit and adjusted her mask. The instructor handed her an oxygen cylinder, and she took a deep breath, letting the cool air fill her lungs. With a final nod, she stepped off the boat and into the crystal-clear water.

As she descended into the depths along with her instructor, the sunlight gradually faded and was replaced by a soft, ethereal glow. She marveled at the vibrant colors of the coral reef, which seemed to stretch out endlessly in every direction. Schools of colorful fish darted through the coral, their scales shimmering in the underwater light.

Sakthi took a deep breath and continued her descent, the weight of her scuba gear pulling her gently downward. There was a beautiful silence. She was in another world, and the peace she felt was something she never knew existed.

Suddenly, a flash of orange caught her eye. Sakthi squinted, trying to focus on the tiny figure darting through the coral. To her delight, she realized it was a Nemo-like clown fish. She chased after the little guy, her heart filled with joy as she explored the underwater world.

As they swam further, Sakthi noticed a dark opening—a mysterious cave in the dark, silent waters, tempting her to explore its depths. She signaled to the instructor, asking him if they could go in. He paused for a moment and then shrugged. Obviously, the situation was not the best place for an elaborate conversation. The fact that he was gliding into the cave seemed like a yes.

With a sense of excitement, she cautiously followed him and entered it. She kept looking back, wondering if she would have time to turn and swim back into the open ocean in case she saw a shark or something. There was no way to communicate with the instructor and ask him about sharks. She convinced herself that she would not be allowed here in the first place if it had been dangerous and kept swimming.

They had not entered a cave but a tunnel. She could see light at the end of it. It was very dim, but it was there. As they swam deeper, the light changed, and Sakthi felt like she was near the center of the Earth. Well, she obviously knew that she wasn't. But the water was very clear and calm, and she could see the fish swimming around her.

She thought to herself, "This is amazing!"

As Sakthi moved deeper into the tunnel, she noticed that the walls were covered with colorful corals and sea plants. She couldn't help but think, "Nature is so beautiful."

It was like being in a dream, and she never wanted it to end. She also saw rock formations and stalactites formed over thousands of years by the slow drip of mineral-rich water. They added to the tunnel's otherworldly beauty, creating a surreal and magical atmosphere. As Sakthi reached the end of the tunnel, she paused for a moment, taking in the beauty around her. It was a fantastic experience, and she knew she would cherish it forever.

When she exited the tunnel, she saw a sunken ship. It was a somber reminder of a past tragedy. Her instructor explained that the ship had sunk during a storm and had remained untouched since then. After being submerged in the water for so long, the ship appeared ancient and weathered, with its metal hull covered in rust and marine growth such as algae, barnacles, and coral. Its once-vibrant colors had faded, and it looked like it had been partially buried in the seabed. This was not surprising as it had been underwater for quite some time.

The waters around the ship were teeming with life as the sunken vessel had become an artificial reef, attracting a variety of marine animals. Fish of all shapes and sizes swam around the ship, using it as a shelter and a feeding ground. Sea plants had attached themselves to the hull, further enhancing its appearance as a natural part of the underwater ecosystem. The sea animals reacted to the ship in different ways. Some used it as a place to hide from predators or as a nesting site. Larger ones such as sharks or rays used it as a hunting ground, attracted by the abundance of smaller fish.

The swim felt like only a few minutes had passed at times and like hours at others. Time had no meaning underwater. Since they didn't live here, both Sakthi and the instructor had to go back to land. Though she was returning with a heavy heart, for her, the boat ride back to the shore was surreal. She kept replaying the brilliant swim and swore to dive at least once a year.

SETTING UP CAMP

A defining moment is a point in your life when you're urged to make a life-altering decision. You experience something that changes you inside out—what you can do, how you see things, how you respond, your choices and actions, and most importantly, what truly matters to you.

For some, it could be a single moment, while for others, it could be like a series of falling dominoes. More often than not, these moments stand out, and you can go back to the exact point in life and say, "There. That's where it all happened."

This is what happened to Sakthi. This was her moment.

It was her last evening on the island, and Sakthi was watching the sunset. The image of the setting sun, which looked like a ripe, well-defined orange, was distorted. Like someone had poked it, and the orange juice had splashed out. The thing about the sun during this time of the evening was that even the slightest change in its shape could be seen from millions of miles away. So, when the comet hit the sun, she could see the impact.

She noticed a teeny-tiny ripple on its surface. The comet seemed to have just given it a little nudge, and suddenly, wild flares were shooting out. Being the sci-fi geek that she was, Sakthi knew exactly what was happening.

Trivia time.

When a comet, which is like a big icy rock, hits the sun, the sun's intense heat causes the ice on the comet to turn into gas. This process releases a lot of energy, creating a bright burst on the sun's surface. This is known as a solar flare. This is like a big fiery splash caused by the comet colliding with the sun's hot atmosphere.

The magnetic energy built up in the sun's atmosphere is released suddenly. Solar flares can release energy equivalent to millions of hydrogen bombs exploding at the same time. They can have various effects on Earth, including disrupting satellite communications, causing power grid fluctuations, and creating beautiful auroras in the polar regions.

As Sakthi fixed her eyes on the spectacle, she couldn't help but think that it was something incredible and terrifying, too. The radiation was like an unstoppable force, swelling up and zooming closer to her, faster than a race car on a hot track. It felt as if it had gripped her like a cosmic hand reaching out and holding her in one place.

And then, BAM! The radiation hit her like a ton of bricks. It didn't pull any punches. Sakthi didn't stand a chance. The world around her turned into a swirl of colors and she was out like a light.

CHAPTER SIX

THE TRANSFORMATION

After a while, Sakthi stirred from the unexpected attack. Confused and blank, she realized that time had played tricks on her—she had either taken a nap, or the clock had sprinted ahead without her knowledge.

With a shudder, she staggered back to her tent and burrowed into her sleeping bag for a little power nap. It was 9:30 PM, and Sakthi felt like she had run a marathon in outer space. However, her journey was far from finished. In fact, it had barely begun.

A gnawing hunger woke her up. She munched on her cheese sandwich, acting like a squirrel with its favorite nut, and the dinner restored her energy. She had no idea what had happened. There was no one around. She knew she looked and felt fine, but something was amiss. She was feeling **too** fine. She had just been hit by a solar flare. It had to have some side effects. On the contrary, the mild body aches from scuba diving had vanished. She felt rejuvenated. She felt like she could do another dive.

Sakthi looked at herself in the mirror after dinner. All was well. Two eyes, one nose, and one mouth. She moved her arms and legs experimentally. Yup. All good. She took a change of clothes, walked to the stream nearby, and dipped her hand in the water. It was warm and perfect. Taking a deep breath, she disrobed and jumped into the water. It felt amazing. After floating for a while, she calmed down. Yes, she was overthinking the whole episode. Nothing had happened. She looked at the skies. Everything was dark. She was surrounded by innocent and endless darkness. Yup. All was well.

She looked at herself again. She was fine. Yet, she could not explain what had happened in the past three hours. The hours she had spent unconscious. What had hit her? Why was she not hurt?

Oh well.

After putting on some dry clothes, she collected the rest of her things and walked back to the tent. She wanted to head back to civilization more than anything else now. She seemed to have spent too much time alone. She had reached that zone and wanted to go home. She hurriedly finished her vlog, packed her bags, and tried to sleep.

But she couldn't. She kept looking at her watch, willing it to go faster. It was like a vessel of milk, which wouldn't boil when you have your eyes on it. Time moved at a snail's pace. At last, it was 2:00 AM, and in five hours, she had to report back to the main camp. Sakthi closed her eyes and started counting sheep. Before she knew it, it was 6:30 AM. The sun was rising. It was fine. It was as though Sakthi had dreamed the whole thing. She did have a wild imagination after all.

That's when she heard a tiny squeak—a fallen bird was struggling to regain its footing. Sakthi rushed to pick it up. Its leg was broken. She had no idea how it had happened. But it had. The bird chirped in pain, and she knew she had to do something.

Sakthi scooped up the little thing, nestling it close to her chest to share her warmth. She wished the bird would heal and its pain would vanish. She held it tight and kissed it. She didn't realize she was tearing up. That's when things got weird. As she held the bird, it started to glow, like a tiny living nightlight. It was as if someone had flicked a switch, and a bulb inside the bird had lit up. But it didn't last long. In less than a minute, the glow faded.

Sakthi slowly uncurled her fingers. She didn't believe what happened next. The little bird let out a chirpy, happy song and jumped out of her palms onto the ground. Before being bathed in the magical glow, the little bird had been physically injured, shivering in pain and fear. Now, it seemed as if the glow had worked a healing spell. The bird was no longer trembling in pain; it was back to its usual lively and energetic self.

Sakthi was more spooked than she'd ever been in her life. The happenings felt like something straight out of a Harry Potter movie, and she had no clue what to make of it. Panic set in, and all she wanted was to retreat to the safety of her tent and shut out the bewildering world.

In the blink of an eye, as if by some otherworldly force, she found herself back inside the tent. But she couldn't explain how she got there. It was like a crazy, topsy-turvy dream that left her head spinning. Nothing added up, and she felt utterly lost and terrified. It was a fear like she'd never experienced before, the kind that crawls under your skin and sends shivers down your spine. Solar flares generally do not affect humans. The Earth's atmosphere makes sure of that. It more or less acts as a shield to prevent cosmic radiation from causing harm.

Well, she was not harmed, was she? But it had given her powers—the power to heal and the power of speed. What else could she do? Only time will tell. She needed to talk to her dad. He would know what to do.

All she knew was that she was no longer the same person. She was someone else. She was something else.

She became Agni.

CHAPTER SEVEN

AGNI

Once Sakthi reached home, she knew she had to be open about her powers with her father. They had a clear policy: no secrets, no hiding anything, no matter what. It was a principle that was ingrained in her, something she not only followed but also loved.

The first thing she did was sit down with him and explain what had happened. He was initially horrified and urged her to visit the village doctor. It was a difficult thing to process. Who would have thought something like this would happen in real life? Thanks to his daughter's passion for this genre, he had seen many superhero movies. But to experience something like this was a different thing altogether. With his own daughter, it was his job to protect her and help her with decisions. But he had no idea where to begin.

He also knew that going to the doctor would attract unnecessary attention, not to mention all the poking and prodding she would have to undergo. He did not want Sakthi to become a showpiece like Exhibit A for superhuman powers. Superman did not hide his identity for the joy of it. It was to ensure he could do what he wanted while keeping his family safe. He didn't want the world to view Clark Kent as a museum piece. Even worse, as a danger to society. So that was ruled out.

There was only one option. Sakthi decided to get her dad to help her adjust to these powers.

Sakthi… I am sorry, Agni, started training with her father, who was a physical education teacher at a local school. His knowledge in this space was limited. But then, did anyone else on the planet know more about such powers? Nope. This was all they had, and it was time to push through.

Day one

Day one was tough. The task seemed easy. But it didn't quite work out the way she wanted.

Sakthi's father broke a twig and asked her to fix it. She held the pieces nervously in her palms, closed them tightly, and waited. At first, nothing happened, and she was puzzled. Then she squeezed her hands harder. She felt a slightly warm sensation running through her palms. But what shocked her was the expression on her father's face. He looked positively horrified. Looking down, she realized her hands were on fire. She rushed to the well and dipped her hands inside the bucket of water that hung there. The fire was put out, and her skin was perfectly fine. In fact, she didn't feel any pain from the flames. However, the heat had caused the twigs to turn black and had charred them completely.

Her dad came running towards the well. He was panting. They had been nearly 75 meters away from the well when her hands had caught fire. They looked at each other but had nothing to say. The silence between them said it all.

They knew that she had three powers: spontaneous combustion, healing, and speed. She could create and control fire and heat with her hands.

They decided to take a break. They needed it!

Day two

Repeat. The second twig was broken into two pieces and handed to her, but her palms again produced sparks. Yup, it was not going as planned.

Day three

Day four

Day five

Day six

Day seven

Agni spent a few days pondering over how she had healed the bird. She remembered feeling sad, anxious, and sorry for the bird. And she had wished for the bird to heal. Yes, that was the difference. While working with the twig, she felt nothing but excitement and fun. There was no intent to cure the twig. It was just a game to test her powers.

She took the two pieces of twig from her father. He also placed three buckets of water nearby. When there is a possibility of fire, you can never have too much water. Don't you agree?

Agni closed her hands and eyes at the same time. She cleared her mind. This was no longer a game. It was something that could make a difference to her in every way. She thought of nothing but the twig and how she would feel once it was whole again.

With a gentle touch and a focused mind, she channeled her healing powers into the twig. To her amazement, the twig began to mend, and the broken ends fused seamlessly. This simple exercise was the beginning of Agni's training to control and hone her healing abilities.

As Agni looked deeper into her powers, she began to wonder about how she could crack the mysteries of her abilities, one extraordinary gift at a time. She kept going through the notes in her head like she was revising for an exam. An exam that she would be writing for the rest of her life.

Her powers could be summarized as:

- **Energy absorption:** Agni could absorb solar energy, which empowered her healing abilities and provided her with a source of energy for other feats.

- **Regeneration:** Her cells could regenerate at an accelerated rate, allowing her to heal from injuries faster.

- **Heat manipulation:** She could control and manipulate heat, using it to heal, create protective barriers, or even as a weapon against enemies.

CHAPTER EIGHT

AGNI'S GROWTH

Agni's path going forward was simple and clear. She stood for human rights and duties. She made sure everyone fulfilled their responsibilities and that their rights were not violated, and fought for those who were denied their basic needs.

When she returned to her usual life, Agni could tell that things were about to get crazy in the best way possible. The people around her had always loved her for her big heart and warm personality. But now, with her newfound powers, they practically put her on a pedestal. It was like she'd become their superhero and a real-life legend.

Telling everyone

Agni remembered telling everyone about her newfound abilities. She had stood at the center of the small square near her house, the evening sun casting long shadows around her. Her heart raced, but she knew the moment was too important to back down. She took a deep breath, feeling the weight of every eye on her. The people she had grown up with—those who had been there for her through everything—deserved to know the truth.

"Sakthi, what's going on?" an elderly woman called out from the crowd, her voice laced with concern. "We've heard rumors… but we don't understand."

Agni swallowed hard, her throat dry. It was time to tell them that Sakthi and Agni were the same person. She looked around at the familiar faces—people who had helped her family when her mother passed away and those who had offered meals and comfort during those dark days. These were her people. Her family.

"I've been hiding something from all of you," Agni began, her voice trembling slightly. "But I can't do that anymore. You've known me my whole life. You've seen me at my worst and my best. You stood by us when my mother… when she left us."

A murmur ran through the crowd, a mixture of curiosity and fear. Agni felt the unease pervading the air like a thick fog. But she pressed on.

"I have powers," she said, the words hanging heavy in the air. "Not just any powers… but ones that could either protect us or cause harm if not used carefully."

The crowd fell silent. For a moment, it felt like time itself had stopped. Agni saw the fear in their eyes, but it wasn't the fear she had dreaded. It was fear for her, not of her.

"Powers?" a middle-aged man, her father's closest friend, stepped forward. "What kind of powers?"

Agni took another deep breath. "The kind that could save lives… or change them forever."

There was a pause before a young mother with a baby in her arms spoke up. "Are you dangerous?"

"No, not to you. Never to you. I want to use what I have to help us all—to protect our home and surroundings."

The crowd exchanged glances, uncertainty flickering in their eyes. But then, slowly, the atmosphere began to shift. The fear in their faces softened and was replaced by something else—understanding, perhaps even admiration.

A few moments passed before the elderly woman spoke again, her voice steady. "We've always known you were special, Sakthi. Maybe we didn't realize just how special. But if you're telling us this now, it's because you trust us. And we trust you."

It was demo time. She showed them what she could do.

One by one, the others nodded, murmuring their agreement. The man who had asked about her powers stepped forward and placed a hand on her shoulder. "We've been through a lot together, Sakthi. From now on, I will call you Agni. We're not about to turn our backs on you."

Agni felt relief wash over her then. With tears stinging her eyes, she realized that they had not been afraid of her. They had understood. And more importantly, they had accepted her for who she was.

"Thank you," Agni whispered, her voice thick with emotion. "I promise I'll use my powers for good—to keep us safe."

From that moment on, things changed.

Back to the present

The people who knew her not only learned to live with Agni's powers but began to appreciate them. They saw her as a protector and someone who could make a real difference in their lives. And for Agni, there was no greater gift than knowing she could finally be herself— no more hiding, no more secrets. Just the truth, shared with the people who mattered the most.

Years went by. Agni wasn't just loved; she was respected. Everyone looked upon her as some kind of Goddess—in a super cool way. It was as if she had stepped right out of a comic book and into their lives. Her powers, which were a secret earlier, now had everyone wide-eyed and amazed. The folks nearby looked at her with awe, as if she'd pulled off the greatest magic trick in history. This was her time. Agni was the star of the show and a source of hope for everyone.

There were many instances where she used her powers to protect her people.

Living near the jungle, there was a fair share of four-legged visitors—monkeys, wild elephants, and even the occasional lion. Now, these wild critters usually kept to themselves. But one lion was different. He had a limp, like he'd been through a showdown with an angry elephant. Nobody dared to get close to that big cat.

But Agni, being all of 24 years old, was enthusiastic and courageous to a fault. She didn't know when to back down. Despite repeated warnings from her elders, she strolled right up to the lion with a mug of water and a cotton cloth. The craziest part was that the lion didn't budge. It was as if he knew she was there to help him.

Agni cleaned his wound with water and applied pressure to stop the bleeding. And then, out of the blue, it happened! A warm, golden glow emerged from her hands like she'd just caught the sun and held it in her palms.

And then, poof, the light vanished, as if someone had just turned off a switch.

Everyone watching the scene fell into a hushed silence. Agni gingerly withdrew her hands, which were soaked in blood, but the big feline's wound had healed completely. He got up, looking just as puzzled as everyone else, gave Agni a grateful lick on the face, and ambled off into the jungle. You can imagine the chaos that followed. Everyone came rushing to hug Agni. It seemed like they'd found a long-lost friend.

Agni helped not only animals but people, too. Without a proper hospital nearby, people from remote corners had to endure all sorts of illnesses and injuries. Agni was their savior, the one who could make things right instantly. She became the answer to all their problems, their very own superhero. But the best part was that she never took any of it for granted. Agni knew that with great powers came even greater responsibilities, and she was more than up for the challenge.

EPILOGUE

The Mysterious Abyss

The entire population was flourishing, and people were smiling with the abundance of the harvest season. Agni, their beloved protector, was the reason behind this prosperity. She was more than a girl; she was everyone's guardian angel. But on this quiet evening, as the sun dipped below the horizon, Agni's gaze was drawn to something unusual near the foot of the towering mountains.

She narrowed her eyes, straining to make out the shadowy shape. A dark hole had appeared in the earth. It was deep, ominous, and growing wider with each passing second. Agni's heart skipped a beat. This wasn't just any hole; it was a gaping chasm. It seemed as if the earth was splitting open.

"Agni! Look!" someone cried out, pointing toward the growing abyss.

Soon, a crowd gathered around her, and murmurs of panic rippled through the air. The ground beneath their feet trembled slightly, and Agni could feel the fear spreading like wildfire. The hole was expanding, its edges crumbling away like something beneath was hungrily devouring the earth.

"What is that?" an elderly man whispered, his voice trembling. "It's growing… it's going to swallow us all!"

Another woman clutching her child to her chest turned to Agni with wide, desperate eyes. "Agni, what do we do? You have to stop it!"

Agni stared into the abyss, her mind racing. For a moment, doubt gripped her. She had never seen anything like this before. What if her powers weren't enough? What if she failed? The once-vibrant city, her home, could be consumed by this dark force, leaving nothing but ruin.

But then, deep within her, something shifted. A new awareness and a stronger connection to her abilities surged through her. She couldn't let fear paralyze her— not now, when everyone needed her most.

She turned to everyone, her voice steady despite the chaos. "Stay back. I'll handle this."

The crowd fell silent, all eyes on Agni as she approached the edge of the chasm. The hole yawned before her like a mouth ready to consume everything in its path. Agni could feel the pull of the darkness, a cold energy that sent a shiver down her spine. But she didn't back away.

"I need you to trust me," Agni said, her voice firm. "Whatever happens, don't come near it."

Everyone nodded, though their faces were etched with worry. Agni took a deep breath, her eyes narrowing with determination. She could sense the energy within the earth, a chaotic force tearing it apart. But she could also sense something else—something she could control.

Without another word, Agni stepped closer to the edge. The people gasped, but she remained calm, her focus unshaken. The chasm seemed to pulse, reacting to her presence. It seemed as if it recognized her power. Agni extended her hands, feeling the energy around her, drawing it in, and letting it flow through her like a river of fire.

Then, with a surge of strength, she leaped into the air and dove into the darkness.

To be continued ….

NOTE TO MY YOUNG READERS

Dear young heroes,

As you reach the end of this adventure, I want to share a message that goes beyond the world of fiction. While the story of Agni, her incredible powers, and her journey to becoming a superhero is a thrilling tale of imagination, it also carries a message about the power within each of you.

In India, our beloved nation, there is something truly extraordinary—the Indian Constitution. It's not a dusty book of laws; it is a living document and a guiding light for our country's future. It is a promise etched with the ink of equality, justice, and freedom for all its citizens. And yet, like Agni in our story, our Constitution's real power lies within its people's hearts and minds—it lies within you.

As the youth of this great nation, you are not just its future; you are its present. You are the torchbearers of change, the architects of progress, and the hope for a brighter tomorrow. India's journey towards becoming a developed and prosperous nation lies in your hands. You have the power to shape the future.

Here's what I encourage you to do:

1. **Embrace education:** Education is your greatest ally. It equips you with knowledge and skills, empowering you to face future challenges. Pursue your studies with diligence, for it is through education that you will unlock your full potential.

2. **Dedication and ambition:** Whether you dream of being a scientist, an artist, a doctor, an engineer, a teacher, or anything else, approach your chosen path with passion and ambition. Every dream you pursue can make a positive impact on our society.

3. **Active participation:** Understand how our government works. Discover how leaders are chosen, policies are made, and laws are enacted. Be an engaged and informed citizen who actively participates in the democratic process. Raise your voice, express your opinions, and take an interest in the decisions that shape our nation.

4. **The power to vote:** Exercise your right to vote when the time comes. Choose leaders committed to the betterment of the nation and its people. Your vote is your voice, and it has the power to shape the direction of your country.

5. **Consider public service:** Some of you may aspire to become civil servants, like IAS officers, IPS officers, or government officials. These roles carry immense responsibilities, but they also offer the opportunity to serve the people of India and work tirelessly towards achieving the goals of our constitution.

Remember, the strength of our nation lies in unity and collective effort. Keep a vigilant eye on the progress of your country, question the status quo, and engage in meaningful discussions about our society. Strive to make India a better place for all its citizens.

The future of India depends on an educated, determined, and ambitious generation—the generation reading these words right now. Together, you have the power to transform India's dreams into reality, to turn the pages of the constitution into vibrant chapters of our nation's history.

You can lead India to even greater heights with your unconditional determination, commitment to education, and spirit of unity. The dreams woven into the fabric of the Constitution await their fulfillment, and it is you who will make them come true.

I have faith in your potential and eagerly anticipate the mission you are set for. You are not just my readers; you are the heroes of India's future. Your actions, aspirations, and collective efforts will shape the destiny of our beloved nation.

With boundless hope, inspiration, and a deep belief in your abilities,

– **Indu**

DARE TO DREAM BEYOND THE ORDINARY!

In this section, I challenge you to envision a future where you shape your country the way you believe it should be. It's time to think outside the box, dream big, and let your creativity soar!

Dream school

- Picture your ideal school of the future. What will it look like, and how will you learn there?

- Describe your dream school. What are the subjects, activities, and teachers it will have?

- How will your dream school help you achieve your goals and dreams?

- What can you do to make your current school a better place for learning?

Superhero powers

- If you had powers like Agni, how would you use them to make India a better place?

- What superhero power will you choose, and how will you use it for the good of your country?

- Can you think of a specific problem in India that can be solved with the help of special powers?

- How will you inspire others to use their unique powers to make positive changes in your society?

Dream community

- Imagine a community where everyone helps and supports each other. What will this community look like?

- Describe your dream community. How do people treat each other, and what do they do to help those in need?

- How will living in a supportive community change how you feel and interact with others?

- What small acts of kindness can you perform to create a more caring community in your neighborhood?

Future leaders

- Think about the qualities you want to see in your future leaders. How should they lead India?

- What qualities and values should your future leaders possess to create a better India?

- Can you name a leader from history who inspires you? Explain why.

- How can you develop the qualities of a future leader in your own life, even as a young reader?

The ambition form

- Imagine a form you need to fill out that defines your goals; what would those be?

- If you had to fill out a form regarding all your ambitions and dreams, what would you write?

- How do you think the shift in focus from caste and religion to personal ambitions can benefit your society?

- What can you do now to achieve your goals and dreams?

Life skills school

- Design a school where you learn essential life skills like communication, problem-solving, and empathy rather than memorizing topics you might never use. What life skills would you want to know?

- What life skills do you believe are the most important for young people to learn in school?

- How will learning these skills help you in your future life and career?

- Can you think of an instance when a life skill like problem-solving or communication could come in handy?

Cleaning up our cities

- Imagine being an active part of your local municipality, working alongside others to clean up and beautify your city. What will this experience be like, and how can you make a difference?

- If you were allowed to join a local group that works on cleaning and improving your city, what role would you take on, and why?

- How will participating in such activities benefit your city and its residents?

- What small actions can you take right now to make your neighborhood cleaner and more beautiful?

Make a copy of these questions. Answer them as and when you can. See how the answers change over time.

Remember, there are no right or wrong answers. However, in life, there are rights and duties that guide your actions and interactions with others. Understanding and respecting human rights and responsibilities are essential in building a just and harmonious society.

So, as you explore these ideas, remember also to know your constitution and your role in upholding these principles.

www.ingramcontent.com/pod-product-compliance
Lightning Source LLC
Chambersburg PA
CBHW021210130726
47988CB00002B/598